Death
and
Mr. Potter

Also by Rae Foley
in Thorndike Large Print

IT'S MURDER, MR. POTTER
THE LAST GAMBLE

Death
and
Mr. Potter

Rae Foley

Thorndike Press • Thorndike, Maine

Library of Congress Cataloging in Publication Data:

Foley, Rae, 1900-
    Death and Mr. Potter.

    Reprint. Originally published: New York : Dodd,
Mead, 1955.
    1. Large type books. I. Title.
    [PS3511.0186D4 1985]   813'.54   85-13183
    ISBN 0-89621-662-4 (alk. paper)

Large Print edition available through arrangement with
Dodd, Mead & Company, New York.

Cover design by Armen Kojoyian.

For MARIE TODD
and a cottage in the woods

Chapter 1

At twenty-eight Mr. Potter was known to his mother's women friends as an exemplary son, which was one reason why Mr. Potter had no women friends of his own.

Amanda Potter, in the intervals between tracing her family tree, had inculcated in him the best of habits. His fair hair clung sleekly to his head, his mild face was as negative as a cipher. His manner was self-effacing to the point of invisibility. Not for Mr. Potter the vulgarity of strident neckties or loudness of voice. He was a creature of duty and a slave to routine. He saw the dentist twice a year and paid his bills the day they fell due. He was scrupulously punctual for appointments. On Sundays he decorously passed the plate in church; on Monday evenings, to please his mother, he worked on genealogy, an activity that had led, as he knew bitterly, to his being known as "Hiram out of Amanda."

Mr. Potter had been trained to fix interested eyes on elderly women while they retailed stories of their youth; he paid visits of consolation to the bereaved and was always equipped with a snowy handkerchief to staunch their tears; he danced with wallflowers and manfully tackled the bores at parties. For twenty-eight years he had been a comfort to his mother and an object lesson to his unregenerate contemporaries.

Now and then, it is true, a hint of laughter in his eyes had vaguely disturbed Amanda Potter. Was it possible, she wondered, that below that placid surface there were depths of which she knew nothing? But the gleam always faded before it touched his lips, the laughing demon who had peered out of Mr. Potter's blue eyes for a moment was sternly banished, and his mother was reassured. It was ridiculous to suppose that there was anything about her own son which she did not know.

Amanda had not been informed of the paper bag in the bottom of a bureau drawer that held a surprising collection of medals; nor had she fully understood the peculiar expression on the face of his commanding officer whom she had asked to tea and who had watched, bemused, the deft and self-effacing manner in which Mr. Potter had passed the cupcakes.

What Mr. Potter longed for in the hidden depths of his shy heart was to follow the path of most resistance. Follow it? Blaze it, by might and main and sheer — though he would have shrunk from the words — brute force.

Not that Mr. Potter was resigned. He lived like a dead leaf in a stagnant pool, waiting for rain to swell the brook and send him swirling into more active waters.

And it rained!

II

The body of Amanda Potter had been removed. To the very last it had looked unyieldingly benign, for no one had ever administered charity with so uncompromising a hand. But, though she was gone, the house on Gramercy Park was aware of her presence still. It was in the heavy bank of flowers and the rows of chairs that had been set up for the services. It was in the musty smell of the long drawing room whose windows were always closed to keep out the shrill voices of children playing inside the tiny park. It was in the furniture, massive, old and enduring.

The furniture had belonged to Amanda's parents and to the parents of her late husband,

Hiram Potter. Hiram and Amanda were not, she had always conceded, pretty names, but they were old and therefore worthy. The same criterion applied to the furnishings in the Gramercy Park house, where indestructibility counted more than aesthetics.

The house, long and narrow, of red brick with a white doorway and long windows, was four stories high and one room wide, with an areaway under the high stoop and a long deep basement. The house faced on the park, which was enclosed by a high fence with locked iron gates; it backed on a minute garden darkened by the towering office building that faced Fourth Avenue and shut out the sun, a drawback compensated for by a skylight roof over the dining room, which extended out beyond the rest of the house.

Here Amanda Potter had presided for thirty years. Now her only son stood at the window waiting for the return of the family from the funeral and the reading of Amanda's will. It was typical of Mr. Potter that he should be the first to return. An anxious sort of promptness governed everything he did. For the first time in his recollection he was alone in the house, for even the servants had gone to pay their last tribute to a mistress who had nearly killed them by kindness.

Being alone was so pleasant a sensation that Mr. Potter felt almost guilty. No longer did the house echo with his mother's deep booming voice. Temporarily, it was free even of the fretful voice of his aunt, Prudence Burkett, and the determinedly youthful voices of his two cousins, Thomas and Deborah, to whom Amanda had given a home after the unlamented death of her sister Prudence's improvident husband. For years, Mr. Potter had regarded his nearest relations with a simple, undeviating loathing. The prospect of booting them all out of the house was a phantasy that had occupied and brightened many of his leisure hours.

Never before had there been the remotest possibility of turning the phantasy into reality, but now Mr. Potter rehearsed in his mind the fiery words that would unburden his heart and free him of his incubuses — incubi? he questioned himself — and let him have the house to himself.

His aunt, Prudence Burkett, was chronically aggrieved. Tall, raw-boned, and tweedy, nature had not designed her to be the plaintive woman she had become. Deprived of her birthright to a solid income by an inexplicable weakness in her youth, she viewed the world around her with sour disapproval. Practically everything that happened was designed for the sole purpose of bringing her discomfort. People existed chiefly to cause her annoyance. This included shopkeepers, servants, and, particularly, the small children who played in the park and whose ill-timed laughter frequently awakened her from her afternoon nap.

Thomas, her son, was a chubby fellow of twenty-six, with thinning hair, near-set eyes, and a manner which his mother found engagingly boyish. Like his mother he had been defrauded by the impecunious Burkett, but he bore it uncomplainingly because his Aunt Amanda made him an allowance sufficient, he declared with his childlike smile, for his simple tastes. When Mr. Potter recalled Thomas's expensive German cameras, the small movie projector and the room fitted up in the basement to show movies, the tailormade suits and handmade shirts and shoes, even he conceded that Thomas Burkett could make a little money go a long way.

Deborah, the daughter, was a faded blonde of twenty-seven, a flower that had begun to wither on the stalk without ever having bloomed. Like Thomas she had an incorrigibly youthful manner, a high girlish voice that was growing sharp, and dresses that would have looked unsophisticated on a highschool girl. Deborah made a career of being delicate and for some weeks she had been the object of her mother's tender solicitude. For Deborah was suffering from a broken heart.

Behind Mr. Potter hung the heavy, cloying odor of flowers in the stale room. Before him was the pocket handkerchief park behind its iron gates. The trees were still stark, the grass was brown, the statue of Edwin Booth, looking cold and lonely, brooded over the Players. From the entrance to the Players emerged Adam Faber, a big ruddy-faced man with heavy white hair and a leonine head. Faber, as everyone knows, had been the literary sensation of 1914 when his verse play, *Flame on the Ground,* was produced. Because no critic had dared admit that he did not know what it meant, the play had had a tremendously enthusiastic press. With this work Faber had purged his bosom of the perilous stuff of creation and he had produced no more. For forty years his only creation had been the personality of Adam Faber and as a result he was worth his weight in gold on Ladies Day at the Players because he looked like a writer, which happens to be a very rare quality indeed. His presence at its portals was almost as fixed as that of Edwin Booth in the park.

The day was bleak and gray but on the paths of the park, under the watchful eyes of nurses,

13

little boys were shooting marbles and little girls tried out roller skates on wobbly ankles. This idyllic scene was marred by several raucous youngsters, unaccompanied by nurses, who, like foxes in a chicken house, were spreading consternation by their uninhibited behavior. One of these looked up to find Mr. Potter peering between the heavy draperies that shrouded the long windows. He made a furtive, conspiratorial signal.

Mr. Potter caught himself looking guiltily over his shoulder before he responded and then remembered that he was alone in the house. On an impulse, he flung wide the window and waved his arm violently. Then, shocked and mortified, he drew back, closed the window and let the heavy draperies fall into place, shutting out the park, shutting in the funereal air of the room.

Mr. Potter had a guilty conscience. The park was reserved for solid citizens who had keys to the big gates but, more than once, he had made a cautious descent on the east gate, farthest from the house, which he had unlocked for waifs from Third Avenue, whose wistful vigil outside the fence was more than he could bear. Some of these intruders were responsible for the violent energy now being unleashed in the park. Theoretically, none of the key-holders objected to juvenile energy; in their secret hearts, however, they wanted the little park to maintain all the picturesqueness of a postcard view — and its silence.

The area door closed and Mr. Potter was no longer alone. Tito and Antonia Petrella, the Italian couple whom Amanda had hired but never tamed, had come home. Tito, Mr. Potter thought enviously, would fortify himself with a large glass of red wine while Antonia made tea and set out little cupcakes for the bereaved relations soon to invade the house.

A car door slammed, there were feet on the stoop and the doorbell rang. Prudence Burkett never carried a key. What, she demanded, were servants for? Mr. Potter sighed and, in order to give Tito time to finish his drink in peace, opened the door himself.

Three men and three women trooped into the hall. Mrs. Burkett led the way upstairs with anxious determination to underline the fact that her status had changed with her sister's death, that henceforth she was the hostess. She was followed by the two younger women. The three men, dropping overcoats, hats and gloves on the beautifully carved chest in the hall, wandered into the drawing room.

With the best will in the world there was no way of combating successfully the funereal atmosphere. The neat rows of folding chairs left no space for anyone to move around and Mr. Potter suggested that they go into the library beyond. This was hardly an improvement because the odor of flowers followed them and the room was, if anything, gloomier than the drawing room. Like the middle room in most New York houses of a past era, it had no windows, and depended entirely on artificial lighting. As Amanda's taste had run to lamps with dark maroon shades, the result was anything but exhilarating.

The men moved around restively, awaiting the descent of the women. Whatever their drawbacks, women were better at this sort of thing. Under the best of circumstances the four men disliked one another heartily and only the solemnity of death in their midst could bring about even an artificial harmony among them.

Thomas Burkett, his chubby face properly grave, hovered for a moment and then retreated inconspicuously to the dining room at the back where, judging by the sound, he was pouring himself a drink. Wilbur Wagstaff, the oldest man present and Amanda's lawyer, was short and overweight, with a habit of standing so erect he almost leaned backward in a losing effort to compensate for his meager number of inches.

Mr. Potter, hovering around helpfully but ineffectually, bent over to light the fire that had been laid in the big white fireplace. A spark shot out of the grate and came to rest on the silky oriental rug. Before he could move, Bernard Fullmer kicked it back accurately into the fire.

Fullmer had the kind of charm that made him a favorite with men as well as women. A spectacular athlete in college, he was already, although a year younger than Mr. Potter, becoming known in New York politics for his courage, his hard driving power and his integrity. Bayard, his supports called him, and not even the opposition laughed at the name. He was that kind of young man.

Mr. Potter watched him somberly, seeing a big fellow with powerful shoulders, good looks that managed to please without being offensive, easy manners, and an unostentatious kind of self-confidence. Fullmer not only represented the things he would like to be; he had also succeeded in placing his solitaire on the finger of the one girl whom Mr. Potter eyed wistfully from afar. Not that he had ever attempted to explain himself to Patricia Wagstaff; he had always known that his vivid, delightful Pat would not look at a colorless individual like himself. Bernard Fullmer, without money, without influence, representing a party hostile not only to her father's convictions but to his interests, had stepped in and captured the unattainable.

Wagstaff and his prospective son-in-law treated one another with formal politeness that did nothing to warm the atmosphere. The pouches in which the lawyer's eyes were imbedded, the self-indulgence of his mouth were in marked contrast to the self-discipline of Fullmer's handsome face. The lawyer made no secret of his passion for gambling. Fullmer was dedicated to cleaning up gambling in all its aspects. Dedicated, Mr. Potter thought, was not an extreme word in Fullmer's case. The youthful politician was incorruptible. It was significant that Wagstaff had been the one to yield; that Fullmer was going to marry Patricia on his own terms; that Patricia, spoiled and self-willed, was putty in her fiancé's hands.

Mr. Potter exchanged platitudes with his guests and hated Bernard Fullmer. Intercepting a glance the lawyer gave his prospective son-in-law, he was startled to see that Wagstaff hated him, too.

It was a relief when the women trooped down the stairs, their voices muted to a pitch suitable for the occasion. Thomas Burkett, chewing a mint, came back hastily from the dining room, pressed his mother's hand and leaned boyishly against her chair. His sister, red eyed and, unfortunately, red nosed, dropped onto a pouf, which she regarded as a girlish action, and drew out a handkerchief in case her emotions, always so susceptible, should be aroused.

Patricia Wagstaff, tall, broad-shouldered for a girl, with tawny hair and eyes, was not, Mr. Potter supposed, beautiful. Her attraction lay in a quality of almost electric aliveness that made her quick gestures, her contralto voice, her eyes, all seem to be giving off sparks. Mr. Potter tried hard not to look at her and ended, as always, by gazing with a doglike devotion that was unnerving.

Deborah, who was uneasy when she was not receiving sympathy, stretched out her hand with a little-girl gesture to Fullmer. His good-looking face flushed as he patted it in a helpless, masculine manner. Patricia, with one of the easy flowing gestures which enchanted Mr. Potter, slipped her hand under her fiancé's arm and grinned with gamine-like malice at the thwarted Deborah.

"The trick," she said, "is to get your man."

"The trick," Deborah said nastily, "is to keep him."

To Mr. Potter's surprise Pat turned white with anger. Her lips were parted for a retort when Fullmer spoke to her in a low tone. She looked at him, checked the words on her lips, and summoned up a smile. A curiously anxious smile. Placating. Like an affectionate puppy that has been scolded.

"Girls," Prudence Burkett said querulously, "how can you joke at a time like this!"

Joke, Mr. Potter thought, was hardly an apt word for the naked antagonism between Patricia and Deborah.

Wagstaff put on his reading glasses, took a sweeping look over them at his attentive audience, and began to read aloud the last will and testament of Amanda Potter.

When he had concluded there was a stricken silence that Mrs. Burkett was the first to break. "Wilbur, I don't pretend to understand legal terminology. Can I possibly be right in supposing that Amanda left everything to Hiram? That her own sister and her sister's children are cut off without a cent?"

Wagstaff gave her a wary glance. "Amanda's estate goes to her son. Quite naturally. But she arranged that, so long as he lives, Hiram will provide you all with a home. And, in case of his death, the estate will be divided equally among you."

"My sister can hardly have expected that I would survive Hiram," Mrs. Burkett said, spots of angry color glowing in her cheeks.

In the ensuing silence, Mr. Potter wrenched his attention away from Patricia Wagstaff and looked around. In three pairs of eyes he read the unmistakable wish that he was dead.

Chapter 2

Never, in all the years of Amanda's reign, had Mr. Potter felt as trapped as he did now when he was master of her fortune and head of her house. She had foisted on him the presence of the three people he most disliked for so long as they all should live.

For the rest of his days he would hear Aunt Prudence ordering Tito to drive small children out of the park to still their laughter; he would reluctantly escort Deborah to concerts and fill in at dances when she became a wallflower, for Deborah clung to the wall like plaster; he would be expected to introduce Thomas to "useful" acquaintances and watch his boyish manner and provide him with a key to his own car.

Antonia, a big woman with enormous breasts, snapping black eyes and a hint of a mustache above her cheerful mouth, brought in a teatray, which, after a moment's hesitation, she placed in front of Prudence Burkett. Even in uniform, Antonia contrived to look sloppy, to arouse apprehensions about the ability of her dress to contain her billowy body without seams giving way here and there.

Mrs. Burkett was temporarily mollified by this recognition of her unchallenged position as mistress of the house. Patricia, gravitating like a magnet to the north toward her fiancé, stood beside him in front of the fireplace, talking in low tones designed only for his ears. Mr. Potter's heart experienced its familiar sensation of having been squeezed by a giant hand at this token of the intimacy and understanding that shut them inside a magic circle, that shut him out.

And yet, he thought, Pat's engagement had changed her. A kind of arrogance in her carriage, in her speech, which had indicated, "I'll do as I please, whether you like it or not," was gone. Obviously, Pat was doing as Fullmer pleased. Her gaiety was tempered by the restraint that was proper for the wife of a public man. A frown, a raise of Fullmer's eyebrows was enough to check her speech, always so uninhibited. Like Alice, Mr. Potter thought, in anger and pity, she trembled with fear at his frown.

Deborah, too, was watching the couple in

front of the fireplace, wincing away from their happiness because she had set her heart on Bernard Fullmer. What rankled most was that neither of them noticed her. Sometimes Mr. Potter wondered whether he would have had a ghost of a chance with Patricia if it had not been for his cousins, for the malice that tinged every word Deborah spoke to her, for the unconcealed dislike that Patricia revealed for Thomas.

Mr. Potter, who noticed everything that happened to Pat, saw that she was watching Thomas covertly even while she talked to Fullmer, and that there was a kind of uneasy question in her tawny eyes. Thomas himself, patting his mother's shoulder — Thomas was a great one for touching people — observed them all with thinly veiled amusement.

Fullmer looked at his watch. "Afraid I'll have to be off," he said, "I have a committee meeting."

"Oh, no, darling!" Pat protested in disappointment.

Wagstaff scowled at Fullmer. Having indulged his only child all her life, he could not endure to see her deprived of anything on which she had set her heart.

"The Crusade can struggle along without you for one day," he said drily.

Fullmer checked what he had been about to say. "The trouble," he said in a deprecating manner, "is that they've arranged this meeting to help blueprint my campaign. These are the men who are backing me. After all, I owe them something."

"How about Pat?" Wagstaff's face was mottled with anger. Pat, in quick alarm, tried to stop him but for once he ignored her. "Spending her days down at that Settlement House to please you. She's not a cause, she's a woman."

For a moment Fullmer smiled faintly at Pat. "I'm well aware of that."

Pat returned his smile with a blinding radiance in her face. "As long as you are aware of that, nothing else matters. Go on to your meeting but call me when it's over. No matter what time."

Deborah's pale eyes were fixed on Fullmer's face, as though she were determined not to miss any indication of his love for Pat. Like pressing on a sore tooth, Mr. Potter thought.

Thomas stroked his sister's cheek with one of his softly cushioned hands on whose fingertips the flesh made little pads. "What we've got to do, little sister, is concentrate on earning an honest living. No Settlement House service for you; unpaid work is for the rich." He let the phrase drop into a pool of silence. Fullmer set his jaw but he made no reply to the suggestion that he was marrying Pat for her money. "As for me," Thomas went on, flashing his boyish smile, "I can always make a living with my camera."

Mr. Potter felt himself stifling. The house had become a prison, a place in which he was to serve a life sentence. Even the presence of Patricia, her bright hair glowing in the dark room, was not enough to keep him in the house. He had to escape, if only for a moment.

Out in the hall, impressive with its lovely staircase, its floor tessellated in black and white marble, its long gilt-edged mirror, he shrugged into a topcoat and reached for the key to the park, which always hung on a hook beside the door. With furtive caution he let himself out and crossed the street like a man in flight.

Twilight was deepening into night and it was almost dark in the little park. Mr. Potter used his pocket lighter to guide him in fitting the big key into the lock, hurrying lest someone look out of the window and observe him making his escape. He was dimly aware of someone standing beside him. The big gate swung open, he went inside, and a girl crowded in behind him. He shut the gate and turned around, startled.

The girl was equally startled when she saw

his face. After a pause she said, "I hope you don't mind. I forgot my key."

"Not at all," Mr. Potter said with mechanical politeness.

He did not know much about girls. In his meager experience they were either too hard to get or too easy. Either way they frightened him. But this girl would hardly have frightened a rabbit. In fact, she was rather like a rabbit, looking as though she'd leap across a flower bed if he made a sudden movement.

"Isn't it rather dark for you here?" he asked dubiously.

"Yes, it is. I didn't expect it to be as black as this. Or as empty."

Mr. Potter touched his forehead in lieu of a hat and wandered off along the main path. Somewhat to his surprise the girl caught up with him and walked along at his side. He wondered how he could get rid of her without being rude. He increased his pace until she was almost trotting to keep up with him. He noticed that she was continually turning to look over her shoulder. If she was as nervous as all that, why on earth didn't she go home? Or was he supposed to know her? He ran over in his mind the friends of his mother who lived on the park and who were likely to have a daughter of this age but he couldn't place her.

He had paused at the south gate where street lights touched the girl's face. Rabbit, he thought again. She was very young, perhaps eighteen, with mousy hair unbecomingly arranged above a pale face with rather stupid eyes and an indeterminate chin. It wasn't a face that conveyed much expression, but such expression as there was could be plainly read. She was frightened. Frightened? She was scared out of such wits as she had. And not because the park was dark and empty. Certainly not because of Mr. Potter. She stood as close to him as she dared.

"Do you live on the park?" Mr. Potter asked.

She abandoned the fiction of the key. "Oh, no, I'm just here on business."

Mr. Potter started to walk on and she followed him.

"I hope you don't mind. Just until he comes."

Mr. Potter was about to say firmly that he'd come into the park for a quiet stroll, unaccompanied. It was her eyes that stopped him. The strain in them. And a curious quality that reminded him of something. A fellow in college who had been used to demonstrate hypnotism. Easily led. Got into a lot of trouble afterwards.

Her face made him faintly sick. The girl, of course, was a born victim.

"Hadn't you better go home?" he asked her.

"I'm waiting for," she hesitated, tried again.

28

"It's for my boss."

"He asked you to meet him here?" Mr. Potter was incredulous.

"He's in trouble. And if I can help out, I'll get a bonus. Anyhow, he's wonderful. My roommate, Opal Reed, thinks I exaggerate. But, of course, she doesn't know him. She says I'm a pushover for anyone who is nice to me."

Opal, Mr. Potter thought, has sense.

"But just the same," the girl hurried on as though silence frightened her, "getting the job that way and all, I never dreamed it would work out so well or I'd have such a person to work for."

By this time Mr. Potter knew he wasn't going to be able to shake her off without ruthlessness. She was going to cling to him, with gentle tenacity, because she was afraid to be alone.

They strolled to the end of the park on the east side and turned back, hearing the distant rumble of the Third Avenue Elevated as it passed. Mr. Potter took another look at the girl. At the curious eyes, the futile chin. Smalltown girl, he thought. Middle western accent. The little fool had probably never been on her own before. She was a sitting duck. God knew what she was mixed up in, what had frightened her.

At last she said, "I think everyone ought to be given a chance, don't you? My stepmother always punished right off and I made up my mind I'd always let people explain first."

She did not seem to require any comment. She nibbled away at her thought like a rabbit with a piece of lettuce. "If I hadn't been working overtime, I'd never have known anything about it. I didn't even know there was anyone in the office when I picked up the telephone and heard that voice. Woman's intuition, I guess."

Mr. Potter felt that he had got lost somewhere. "Intuition?"

"The voice sounded so nice and yet I knew at once, even before I understood what it was saying, that it wasn't really nice at all. Why, it was nothing more or less than blackmail!"

Mr. Potter was startled. "Blackmail!"

"Well," she said in her small, flat voice, "if you heard someone say, 'If you don't want it made public, you'll have to pay up by tomorrow,' wouldn't you think it was blackmail?"

"Look here," Mr. Potter said firmly, "you'd better go right straight home. You might get mixed up in something that's too big for you to handle alone."

"I don't know what else to do. Anyhow, a bonus would be some money of my own. And I'm not taking any risk." After a moment she added dubiously, "I guess."

"Why did you follow me in here?"

"I saw you come out of that house. I thought —"

"You mean you were to meet someone from that house?"

Her eyes were fixed. They looked at the tip of his nose. "I thought — you'd have a key. I was tired of standing outside the gate."

Even then he knew that he should have insisted on a truthful answer. It was her defenselessness that checked him. "Who are you?" he asked.

"My name is Jennie Newcomb."

"Look here, Jennie," Mr. Potter said earnestly, "blackmail is an ugly business and the people who do it are apt to be ugly people. You let your boss take care of his own troubles. In fact, you'd better get yourself a new boss."

They were standing at the gate on the north side of the park. The Chrysler Building at Forty-second Street gleamed with light. A bus turned on Twenty-third Street and a taxi stopped at the Gramercy Park Hotel.

Jennie turned to give him a sidelong look. "But if it works out all right, there will be a bonus."

"And if it doesn't work out all right?"

Those horribly suggestible eyes wavered. Jennie was not a girl to cope with conflicting ideas.

31

"Well, what would you do?" she demanded. She stood like a dog watching for a stick to be thrown. "I think you'd wait to see," she said with the first confidence he had heard in her voice. "You wouldn't run away."

This was an accolade of the first water, one Mr. Potter would not have exchanged for any gift he could imagine. No one, except during his unexpectedly aggressive military service, had ever assumed that he was a man to be relied on in time of stress, a man of action. A glow ran through his veins and Mr. Potter lifted his head with proud humility in recognition of the magnificent compliment. Even if it came from this colorless rabbit of a girl.

They walked on, came back to the west gate and stood looking in silence at the gracious lines of the Potter house, at the wreath of white carnations that still hung on the door, reminding them that it was a house of death. Unbidden, some lines from a contemporary poem came to Mr. Potter's mind:

We come in by a terrible gate.
We go out by a terrible gate.

"It's a beautiful house," Jennie said with heartfelt admiration that held no trace of envy. "It must be wonderful to live there."

Thinking of Aunt Prudence, of Thomas, of Deborah, Mr. Potter shuddered. Belatedly, he recalled that the Wagstaffs and Pat's fiancé still waited for him, that he must think of a suitable excuse for his absence.

"I must get back," he said with a sigh and unlocked the gate. "Coming, Jennie?"

For a moment she hesitated, tempted by the open gate, fearful of the shadows in the park at her back, fearful of something else. Then she shook her head. "I've got to wait."

He was surprised to discover how reluctant he was to leave her there.

"I'll be all right," she said.

"You can't get out without a key, you know."

"Someone is coming for me."

"If he shouldn't come, just stand at the gate and yell for Tito. He'll let you out. And tell your boss to handle his own problems."

"You are very kind," she said.

"Good night, Jennie."

"Good night."

The gate clanged shut behind him. Mr. Potter crossed the street and ran up the steps to his front door. Before going in he looked back. Jennie was only a dark shadow beside the darker shadow of a tree.

Chapter 3

After the departure of the Wagstaffs and Full-mer, Mr. Potter went up to his own room to escape the accusing eyes of the Burketts. If they were going to lament the fact that his mother had not left them financially inde-pendent, he preferred to have them do it in his absence. He realized, of course, that he was merely postponing the evil moment. Sooner or later he would have to face their reproaches.

He was aroused from his gloomy meditations by Tito who knocked on the door and came in without waiting for an answer. He carried a small tray with a cocktail glass and a shaker that was beaded with moisture. Mr. Potter eyed him suspiciously. Tito's delicate attentions were apt to serve as a prelude for voicing his grievances.

The middle-aged Italian with a round face, a retreating hair line and a rapidly advancing body, set down the tray. When he had caught Mr. Potter's eye and was sure of his full attention, he flung out his arms in a dramatic gesture.

"This," he declared with the fervor of an operatic tenor, "is the end!"

"Now what is it?" Mr. Potter inquired mildly. Tito had come to the end so frequently that Mr. Potter's mental picture of him was that of a man dangling from the last inch of rope.

"Mrs. Burkett," Tito began. "I am accustomed to her calling me: 'Tito, there's a strange man loitering outside the house; send him away. Tito, call the police; the children in the park are making too much noise.' But at twilight — 'Tito,' she says to me, 'Tito, do you see those birds?'"

Mr. Potter choked and hastily set down his glass.

"I say, 'Mrs. Burkett,'" Tito's arms went wide in a frenzied gesture, "'Mrs. Burkett, it is spring!'"

Mr. Potter stifled his gusts of laughter as best he could until it occurred to him that such uninhibited, irresponsible mirth was unseemly on the night of his mother's funeral. Sobered, he turned around to the waiting and still passionately indignant Tito.

"From now on," he said in his usual quiet, unstressed voice, "the children in the park are to be let alone. If Mrs. Burkett ever again asks you to call the police about them, refer her to me."

Tito's eyes opened wide. Who would ever have believed that Mr. Potter would stand up to his aunt?

"As for the birds," Mr. Potter's voice got hopelessly out of control. At length he managed to say, "Let nature take its course."

Tito still waited, pregnant with communication. "Mrs. Burkett says she's going to move down to Mrs. Potter's room. It will save her one flight of stairs."

Mr. Potter's eyebrows arched but he made no comment and Tito sighed to himself. It was too much to expect that he would put up a fight for his own rights. It was also a pity, because for all his namby-pamby ways, as he and Antonia had agreed only that afternoon, Mr. Potter was a kindly person, which was more than could be said for any of the Burketts.

"They are already at dinner," he said. "Waiting for you."

Mr. Potter groaned, gulped down his drink, and got up to brush his hair. As he came out of his room, always dim and depressing because it was on the rear of the second floor, he thought of the more spacious room on the front, a room which was washed with the morning sun.

Amanda had gone forever. Tomorrow, Aunt Prudence would move into the empty room, into the empty place. He stood in the doorway, whistling tonelessly to himself.

The dining room was at the back of the main hall, built out beyond Mr. Potter's bedroom and roofed by a skylight to compensate for the high office building on Fourth Avenue that shut out the sun. As he started to open the dining room door Mr. Potter heard his cousin Deborah's high voice.

". . . hate to see Bernard Fullmer taken in. I don't believe he's at all in love with Pat and, heaven knows, she is not the kind of wife for a man in politics. She has always been wild and, if you ask me, she always will be. And her father lets her have anything she wants, no matter what. Maybe he can't help himself. She never gives up when she wants something. Remember how she wouldn't eat for three days until he bought her that convertible? And she was only sixteen."

"She's spoiled, all right," Prudence said. "But parents do want their children to have what they want. I'd do a great deal to give you and Thomas the things you'd enjoy. A mother's heart—"

Deborah had no interest to spare in a mother's heart when accompanied by an empty purse.

"A scandal would ruin Bernard's career. But a lot Pat cares. Only she'll learn one thing. He'd drop her in a moment if he thought she'd hurt his career. He has a duty that's more important—"

Thomas snorted.

"Laugh if you want. You don't understand men like Bernard. Neither does Pat. She'd better watch her step, that's all. It would be a nice thing for Bernard if that story about Rod Miller ever came out."

"What story?" her mother demanded alertly. "And who is Rod Miller?"

"He was a gangster," Deborah said. "Pat eloped with him. Mr. Wagstaff found out and the marriage was annulled. Probably it doesn't matter so much now, because Miller is dead. He was killed in some gang war."

"You talk too much, Deb," her brother informed her and, although his voice was pleasant enough, Deborah fell silent.

I don't believe it, Mr. Potter told himself firmly. His gay, vivid Pat, his irreproachable Pat, the girl he hardly dared let himself think of. Belonging to a gangster. Wanting to belong to a gangster. It's all malice, he tried to comfort himself; Deborah hates Pat because of Fullmer. But none the less, he felt curiously sick.

He opened the door and went into the dining

38

room. Already the Burkett influence was crowding out the Potter influence. His aunt had taken his mother's chair at the head of the table. The big crystal chandelier his mother had loved — "I like to see what I eat," she had declared stoutly — was unlighted and his aunt had substituted candles so that there were twelve small pinpoints of light amid the encircling gloom. The drapes had not been drawn and beyond the windows were scattered squares of light in the tall office building, and through the skylight the milky glow of the moon.

"We didn't wait for you," Mrs. Burkett said in the querulous tone that attempted to sound patient and yet to imply martyrdom.

"That's fine," Mr. Potter said, "I was a bit late because I've been planning." He unfolded his napkin. "I want to have the painters in. When mother's room has been redecorated and refurnished I think it will make rather a cheerful study." He helped himself to olives and celery without looking up.

The silence was prolonged. Then Mrs. Burkett said, "While you are making so many changes in your mother's house, I do wish you would install an elevator. The stairs are beginning to be almost more than I can manage."

Mr. Potter looked up to find three pairs of eyes watching him steadily and again he had the curious, chilling sensation he had experienced earlier that day. Then something pulled his eyes up, a thread of sound, a faint cry.

At first, he saw only something dark that blotted out the moon, and then there was a heavy jarring sound. Something had fallen against the hideous fountain Amanda had installed at the end of her formal tree-lined path.

Mr. Potter's chair went over as he leaped toward the French doors that opened on the garden. He ran across the small, neat patch of lawn. Inside, the big chandelier had been switched on and light touched the smug cupid who stood above the fountain, and the body fallen, like Icarus, out of the sky, arms and legs flung out, one leg twisted almost upside down, the head so turned that it was obvious the neck must be broken.

The three Burketts had joined Mr. Potter by now, although he shouted at them to go back to the house. "Don't look at her, Aunt Prudence," he warned the older woman. "Thomas, take them away."

He did not try to see the hidden face. The condition of the head was horrible enough. And he knew, without looking, who she was. He had seen that scarf tied around the girl's head earlier in the evening. Only it had been white then. But the fringe, even with the ghastly muck on it, was the same. Jennie Newcomb had come, literally, to a sticky end. This was the bonus she had earned.

Antonia, running out from the kitchen, added her voice to those of the other two women. "Mother of God!" she screamed. "Mother of God!"

Tito pounded up the stairs from the basement where the Petrellas lived. Mr. Potter moved back from the broken body, shuddering as he saw the great splash of wet blood against the rim of the white fountain. I shouldn't have left her there alone, he thought. I knew that at the time. She was in danger and I was as aware of it as she was. More aware. Because Jennie was born to be a victim.

"Tito," he said without looking around, his voice hoarse and unrecognizable to his own ears, "get the police and turn on the garden floodlight. They'll need it. Thomas, if Deborah doesn't stop screaming, slap her. Hard. Aunt Prudence, you'd better go into the house."

Deborah's incipient hysterics stopped short at his words but she continued to whimper to herself. She did not, however, follow her mother out of the garden. Some sort of morbid fascination held her rooted beside the fountain with its gruesome stain, the smashed body, the head that had split like a ripe melon.

Thomas moved, came to stand beside Mr. Potter. Something in the perennially boyish expression changed, was not boyish at all — was what? Mr. Potter wondered what he had seen for a moment, something that had peered out of his cousin's eyes and hastily vanished. Recognition. Recognition and fear. Thomas's plump hand moved forward, the padded fingertips trembling.

"Don't touch anything!" Mr. Potter warned him.

Thomas's plump hand retreated. "I see," he said nastily, "that you have become the head of the house."

Mr. Potter swiveled around to look at his cousin, wondering whether his own face was as gray. "You," he said, "haven't seen anything yet."

"Boys," Deborah whimpered, "must you quarrel at a time like this?"

The doorbell rang and heavy feet tramped down the hallway and out into the garden. At the same moment the dark garden was flooded with light. As the details became clearer Mr. Potter's stomach heaved. He looked up, tipping his head far back, scanning the windows of the big office building. From one of them Jennie had fallen. But which?

Then the police took over and Mr. Potter's

heart sank. The man in front was O'Toole, driver of the radio car which regularly patrolled the Gramercy Park district and a man who, in a forthright but inexplicable way, hated Mr. Potter. Tall, broad-shouldered, trim in his uniform, the officer was as good looking as Fullmer. If his features were not so regular, his expression was more winning because he was less conscious of its effect. Women getting parking tickets from O'Toole always ended the transaction by smiling back. Young, ambitious and inclined to be pleased with his world. Except when he looked at Mr. Potter. Then his good-humored mouth acquired what could only be termed a snarl.

He stood looking over the scene, the bloodstained fountain, the girl's crumpled body in the flower bed. As he observed her more closely his fresh color faded and he muttered something under his breath. Then he, too, looked up the side of the building. At length he turned to scrutinize Mr. Potter. If it weren't impossible for anyone in the house to have killed her, Mr. Potter thought, he would like to blame me for it.

O'Toole listened to Mr. Potter's account and then sent a man into the library to use the telephone.

"Anyone know who she is?" he asked.

Deborah gave a girlish scream of protest. Thomas looking suitable downcast, shook his head. Mr. Potter eyed his cousin sharply. Inconceivable as it seemed, Thomas had made a quick recovery. He was no longer afraid. He was pleased. Mr. Potter could not mistake the signs. He had seen them too often as a child when he had been punished as a result of hints discreetly dropped by his cousin. Thomas was pleased because someone was in trouble. But who? Jennie? Mr. Potter himself? Someone else? A spasm of rage closed his throat. Thomas knew who Jennie was. Thomas knew who had killed her.

II

The doctor, photographers and police were gone. The press had driven off. The body of Jennie Newcomb had been carried through the house that she had thought would be so lovely to live in.

Thomas had switched on the radio. An unknown girl, the announcer said briskly, had jumped or been pushed from a window of a business building on Fourth Avenue. The girl had fallen into the garden of the Gramercy Park home of Mr. Hiram Potter. The historical

44

old mansion was separated from the office building only by an alley and a small garden. Preliminary inquiries had failed to indicate who she was, and the night watchman declared that he had seen no one of her description in the building. So far it was not known from what window she had fallen. The police had found several open and cleaning women declared that they had closed at least two more while sweeping out the offices. Mrs. Amanda Potter, mother of the man at whose home the tragedy occurred, was buried this afternoon. The Hiram Potters, long influential in New York society. . . .

Thomas turned off the radio. His mother clutched his arm as he got to his feet. "Thomas, you aren't going out tonight, after all that's happened? Please—"

He leaned over her cajolingly, his plump hand patting her cheek. His youthful smile might be that of a naughty boy of ten.

"Just for an hour," he said. "Please let your little boy play for an hour."

Nausea welled up in Mr. Potter but Mrs. Burkett produced an indulgent smile. "You're a bad boy," she said. "Don't be late."

The telephone rang constantly. To be on the fringes of violent death, to know someone who actually saw it happen, lured out of their silence people of whom Mr. Potter had not heard for years.

In between calls his thoughts went around like a cog railway. Someone had murdered Jennie and he did not know what to do about it because his own cousin had some knowledge he had not revealed. Whatever his own estimation of Thomas, he could not throw him to the wolves without giving him a chance. Anyhow, he had no evidence, nothing but a fleeting expression to go on. A fine impression that would make on the police. And O'Toole, for reasons Mr. Potter could not fathom, was hostile. I'll have to watch my step with him, Mr. Potter thought.

He tried not to picture Jennie falling from a great height, her broken body crashing into the dark garden. She had been so afraid of the dark. He hoped she had been unconscious when she went out of the window. The words of the poem came back: We go out by a terrible gate. A terrible gate. A terrible gate.

The only bright moment was when Pat Wagstaff telephoned, her gay voice subdued to the occasion.

"Oh, Hiram, I heard it over the radio. How awful for you!"

He told her what had happened as briefly as possible. If his aunt and Deborah had not been listening to every word, he would have poured out the whole story of Jennie, but it was not advisable to say anything with those avid ears gathering in every word.

"I'm so sorry," Pat said. "Please give Mrs. Burkett my sympathy, will you? And Bernard's too . . . Oh, he's fine, thank you. He's here with me. We wondered what really happened, you know."

Deborah's habitually drooping lips were lifted in a smile. "First time Pat ever called you, Hiram," she said with innate cruelty. "Now you've come into the money she is getting interested."

"Let Pat alone," Mr. Potter said.

"*Sans peur et sans reproche?*" Deborah mocked him. "Look, Hiram, it's all right for old Wagstaff to think she is perfect and to be guarded like a piece of fine china. I never knew a rake who wasn't particular about his own women folks." She added viciously, "And taken in by them. But that girl had been around. I could tell you—"

"But you won't," Mr. Potter said evenly. "You won't, Deborah. Or God help you!"

"Really, Hiram," Mrs. Burkett protested. "I don't know what your mother would say. You forget you are speaking to your own cousin."

"I'm perfectly aware of it. I warn you, Deb-

47

orah, keep your malicous tongue off Pat!"

"If Thomas were here you wouldn't dare speak to defenseless women in that tone," his aunt declared. "I might as well tell you now that I don't like the attitude you have assumed today. It's a trifle ridiculous, isn't it, for you to start acting like the head of the house?"

"I don't see why," Mr. Potter admitted. "After all, I am the head of the house." He went out of the drawing room without waiting for her reply. In the hall he picked up his overcoat and hat, still lying on the chest where he had dropped them when he had come back from his encounter with Jennie in the park.

Deborah came running out to the hall. "Hiram, where are you going?"

He looked at her for a moment and then, without a word, he turned and let himself quietly out of the house.

Chapter 4

For a moment Mr. Potter stood breathing in the fresh cool air, his eyes fixed on the spot inside the gates where he had last seen Jennie. Someone had made an appointment with her in the park. That meant someone to whom a park key was available, someone who lived on one of the four sides of the square that enclosed the park. When he included the hotels and large apartment buildings, it took in a great deal of territory, hundreds of people, but he could narrow it down greatly. There was only one key for each building, regardless of the number of tenants. Anyone wanting to have the gates unlocked must ask the doorman of his building in whose possession the key was required to remain. Therefore, the presence in the park of anyone from a multiple dwelling would be a matter of record. Risky, Mr. Potter thought. Very risky. That left two private homes on the Square and the other one was temporarily closed while its owner was abroad.

Mr. Potter let himself in the house again, moving quietly, and reached for the park key. It was not hanging on its customary hook inside the door, though he distinctly remembered returning it when he had come back from his encounter with Jennie. There was, he cautioned himself quickly, no sense in getting in a panic. The key had been mislaid, that was all. He went through all his pockets and then, hoping his aunt and Deborah would not notice him, passed the open drawing room door noiselessly and went down the back stairs to the Petrellas' room in the basement. Tito, in shirt sleeves, was reading an evening paper, a glass of red wine beside him. He got up when Mr. Potter appeared and reached for his coat.

"Don't bother," Mr. Potter said. "I just want the park key."

"I haven't seen it."

Mr. Potter started to speak, changed his mind.

"You all right?" Tito asked quickly. "You're sick looking."

"I feel sick," Mr. Potter said grimly. He remembered Jennie's words: "I saw you come out of that house. I thought—" She had thought he was the man she was expecting. Thomas, then?

Thomas, who had recognized her? But Thomas had been at the dinner table when the girl fell.

Mr. Potter let himself out through the areaway and looked for his big sedan, which should be at the curb. It was not often that he drove the sedan himself. His mother had felt it was only fair to let the Burketts share the use of the car, and Thomas, in his boyishly irresponsible manner, had practically appropriated it. He must have taken it tonight.

Mr. Potter strolled over to Madison Avenue and began to walk slowly uptown, barely aware of the direction he had taken; concerned with the implications of the missing key and with his own responsibility in the matter. The girl had been murdered and he did not intend to let the murderer get away with it. What could he do? What, after all, did he know about her?

He knew her name, for one thing. Jennie Newcomb. The police did not know that. He knew that she had, or had had, a stepmother who punished without waiting to hear any explanations or excuses. He knew that she had a roommate named Opal Reed. Curious how well he remembered. He knew that she had a boss who was wonderful and who was being blackmailed. He knew that she had had an appointment in the park. An appointment with a man. That was why she had been so startled when he turned out to be the wrong man. And the key to the park was gone from its usual hook. It seemed horribly plausible that someone had come from his own house, the house she had been watching.

He thought over the possibilities: Wilbur Wagstaff, Bernard Fullmer, and his own cousin Thomas, who had certainly known who Jennie was. But Thomas had not attempted to leave the house until after the girl's death. Bernard Fullmer had been insistent on going early because of an appointment.

Mr. Potter slowed to a stop. Bernard Fullmer. If Jennie had been right about the blackmail and she probably had been right for someone to mete out death so promptly, Fullmer was in the most vulnerable position, with plans for a political career under way, his campaign based on his integrity. Bayard with a skeleton in the closet — it would hardly do. Certainly he could have removed the park key from its hook, unobserved. But so, Mr. Potter realized with discouragement, could anyone else.

Murder and Bernard Fullmer! If he were the guilty man, Pat would be free. To what lengths would the man go to protect his reputation, to safeguard his political advancement? Deborah believed he was capable of sacrificing Pat for his career but Deborah might be indulging in a lot of wishful thinking. Like himself, Mr. Potter admitted a little sheepishly.

What do I do first? he wondered. He went into a drugstore, found the telephone booths and opened the Manhattan directory. There was no telephone listed under Jennie Newcomb's name but there was a number for an Opal Reed on West Eighth Street. It was nearly eleven o'clock, an inexcusable hour to call an unknown woman, but then the circumstances were exceptional. He got coins at the counter and dialed the number.

A girl's voice answered quickly, as though she had been waiting for the phone to ring.

"Is this Miss Opal Reed?"

"Yes." She sounded disappointed.

"Is — Miss Newcomb there?"

"No," the girl said in a kind of wail. "I don't know where Jennie is. She hasn't come home. Who is this speaking?"

The right Opal Reed, he thought in satisfaction. "My name is Potter. I wonder if you'd let me come down and see you for a few minutes. I could be there in a quarter of an hour."

"Whatever you're selling, Mister, you're wasting your time."

"I want to talk to you about your friend Jennie."

"Do you know where Jennie is?" she demanded eagerly.

He thought of a broken body on a cold slab. "I'm – afraid so."

There was a pause. Then the girl said, "Look, my boy friend doesn't like having me make dates with anyone else. I'll have to telephone him. Will you call me back in ten minutes?"

For ten minutes Mr. Potter watched in rising alarm while two young girls at the lunch counter made a belated supper of chili and chocolate sundaes. Then he dialed the number again.

This time the girl spoke briskly. "My boy friend says it's all right for you to come if he's here. It'll take him about half an hour." She added, "We'll meet at the Gink Club."

"The – what?"

"The Gink Club. On Eighth Street. We'll be waiting for you just inside the door."

The thought of attempting to speak to a strange woman, perhaps getting the wrong one, in a place where he was completely unknown and his intentions might be suspect, paralyzed Mr. Potter. How, he asked in some trepidation, would he recognize her?

"I'll be wearing a red corduroy coat," she said, "and carrying a perfectly immense black patent leather handbag."

Mr. Potter walked over to Fifth Avenue and

down to Eighth Street, grateful that however drastically Washington Square was changing in the interests of higher education, the Washington Arch was still the same. On Eighth Street, the main stem of Greenwich Village, he turned right, looking for the Gink Club. The sign was so inconspicuous and so shabby that, if he had not been scanning every building carefully, he would have missed it. He eyed the doorway dubiously. It was dark, with a small dingy foyer which, at a pinch, would have held four people standing close together, a row of bells with flyspecked cards above them to indicate the tenants in the rooms above, and a dirty narrow staircase. On the left was a door with a heavy curtain over the glass and a sign: Gink Club.

Mr. Potter opened the door and went in. The room was long and narrow, dark and smoky and noisy. Along the left wall in front ran a long bar, while the room beyond was about three times the width of the front, darker and noisier.

His eyes traveled to a couple perched on bar stools near the door and watching him in the long mirror behind the bar. The girl wore a red corduroy coat and carried a mammoth black patent leather handbag. She was young, not more than twenty, with the figure of a Hollywood starlet, steady brown eyes and an attractive face. Even the sweeping line of lipstick that disfigured her mouth could not altogether conceal its humor, its generosity.

The man with her was about Mr. Potter's age and looked like an amiable college professor, with a round face and round glasses, a briefcase tucked under his arm. He aroused Mr. Potter's interest at once because of his resemblance to a pleasant fellow in the army who had conned a number of trusting soldiers out of their pay.

"Miss Reed?" Mr. Potter asked tentatively.

"I am Opal Reed. This is Dr. Trumble."

Dr. Trumble slid off the bar stool and shook hands.

Mr. Potter looked around. "Any place where we can talk privately?" he asked.

Opal and Dr. Trumble exchanged glances. Then the latter paid his check, neatly wiped the stem of his cocktail glass with his handkerchief, absently wiped the bar in front of his stool, and led the way to a booth at the back of the room.

They sat down and, at Mr. Potter's suggestion, ordered another round of drinks. Only when the glasses were before them and the waiter had gone away, did Mr. Potter turn gravely to the girl.

"I'm so glad you have a friend with you," he

began, "because I'm awfully afraid I have bad news."

"Jennie? I'm nearly frantic. She has never been out so late by herself before and I can't imagine where she would go without telling me. She doesn't even have a boy friend."

"Do you know her well?" Mr. Potter asked, wondering what had drawn together two girls utterly unlike.

Opal's lips curved in affectionate amusement. "You couldn't know Jennie for a day without knowing her well. You can see what she's like at once. She's my roommate. I met her through Sam here. They grew up in the same small town and she called him when she came to New York. She was scared stiff of the big city so I took her in. How did you get my name?"

"She told me about you." Mr. Potter cleared his throat. This was going to be hard to do, and he hated discussing Jennie's death in the furtive atmosphere of this murky room.

He told Opal about going into the park and how Jennie had slipped in after him. He told her about their conversation.

Opal nodded. "That sounds like Jennie, all right; she'll do whatever she's told. She's a nice kid but dumb. She shouldn't be allowed out alone."

"Blackmail," Dr. Trumble said thoughtfully.

"I don't like any part of this."

Mr. Potter went on to the body that had hurtled out of the night into his garden, the body that had been Jennie Newcomb's.

"I heard that over the radio," Opal said in a chocked voice. "But Jennie—" She pushed out her hands as though thrusting away an intolerable picture. "Not Jennie! She wouldn't hurt anyone. The poor little dope." Tears rolled down her cheeks but she did not become hysterical. Mr. Potter's respect for her went up several notches. Opal turned blindly to Dr. Trumble who gathered her into his arms and rocked her gently, murmuring, "There, sugar; there, sugar," but the round face above her head was grim. The round glasses reflected back the light so Mr. Potter could not see the expression in his eyes.

"I think," Mr. Potter said hesitantly, "you ought to see the — body, just to be sure. Though I am afraid there is no real doubt."

Opal Reed shuddered convulsively and then pulled herself out of Dr. Trumble's comforting embrace.

"I'll go," she said. "And I'm going to find the man who did this to a helpless kid."

Dr. Trumble's hand closed over hers. "Just a minute," he said evenly to Mr. Potter. "If you knew her name, how come the police haven't

58

been able to identify her?"

Mr. Potter hesitated but he could not turn back now. He told them about his cousin's look of recognition. And then, having gone so far, he told them about the missing key to the park.

"I figured I might have a better chance of getting the facts out of Thomas — that is, if he does know something about Jennie."

"What made you feel you could handle him better than the police?" Dr. Trumble asked, studying Mr. Potter through the round glasses with the shiny surface.

"He hasn't a penny of his own," Mr. Potter explained. "He is dependent on me now for an allowance. That's not, perhaps, the cleanest weapon I could use but Jennie—"

"So," Trumble said thoughtfully, "you think someone in your house killed her."

"Someone from my house took the park key. That's as far as I can go."

"And why are you getting yourself involved? What's the pitch?"

"She was a sitting duck. And I shouldn't have left her alone in the park. I knew she'd tangled with something she couldn't handle. I feel partly responsible."

For a long time Dr. Trumble studied Mr. Potter. Then he said, almost gently, "Count us in. Opal and I will help. I've known the poor kid almost all her life. Lived in the same small town. And blackmail's a nasty thing. I don't know how to be tactful about this, Mr. Potter. Do you think your cousin was the blackmailer?"

Mr. Potter's horrified protest died in his throat, unuttered. Thomas Burkett a blackmailer! Thomas who made a little money go a long way. Thomas who was always in funds. What had he said after Wagstaff read the will? Something about making a living with his camera, although he was not professional in his standards. His camera, like all his hobbies, would never earn him a living if he used it legitimately.

"It's possible," he said reluctantly.

"That wouldn't stop you?"

"It wouldn't stop me," Mr. Potter assured him.

"You know," Opal said frankly if untactfully, "there's more to you than a person would think." Her face crumpled again. "Poor Jennie! And she thought the sun rose and set in her boss."

"Who is he?" Mr. Potter asked.

"I don't know. She told me the job was confidential. She wasn't allowed to talk about it. Even to me."

Mr. Potter set down his glass, staring. "You don't know!"

Opal shook her head. "Jennie never told me. It was a secret."

"I thought she was in an office somewhere. A kind of clerk," put in Sam Trumble. "No one told me—"

"She made me promise, Sam. I didn't like it but she was so sure it would work out all right. Marvelous in fact."

"But how did she get the job?" Sam asked. "Through an employment agency? An advertisement?"

Opal was frowning as she tried to remember. "I don't think so. There was something queer about it. She just came in one afternoon, all triumphant, and said she'd got a wonderful job in the strangest—"

Opal broke off, staring, alert. There was a good deal of noise at the bar, voices were raised in protest. Three policemen were making their way into the back room and here and there people were pushing back their chairs in response to a summons.

"It's a raid," she said in a whisper.

"Keep your shirt on. We'll get out the back way." Sam Trumble got to his feet, pulling the girl with him. But before leaving, he wiped the table and bench carefully with his handkerchief, polished the glass from which he had been drinking.

Mr. Potter rose automatically to follow them. They pushed open the swinging door into the kitchen and Sam muttered under his breath. He had encountered an obstruction, a bulky obstruction in a blue uniform. The obstruction was pleased.

"Well, if it isn't my old friend Sam!" An amiable hand closed over Sam's arm, a gratified eye was turned on Opal, wandered to Mr. Potter. "In kind of a hurry, aren't you?" the voice said jovially. "Want to get out the back way? No, I don't think so. We're all going together, see? More friendly that way."

In a daze, Mr. Potter the impeccable, the innocent, found himself herded into line and following Sam, Opal, and three or four vociferously indignant patrols through the Gink Club, out the door into Eighth Street, and pushed into the back of a truck-like affair with benches on either side. A grilled door was snapped in his face.

Chapter 5

The next hour was always a little vague to Mr. Potter because it was incredible. There was a confused impression of being told to move along, to save it for the judge; of seeing a great many people who were dejected or frightened or belligerent; of a startled reporter recognizing him and dashing to a telephone; of making a call to Wilbur Wagstaff who, after a thunderstruck ejaculation, had inexplicably laughed.

Wagstaff arrived quickly, listened to the charge and turned to give Mr. Potter an unfathomable look. After a few moments of low-toned conversation he nodded.

"All right, Hiram, come along. You aren't wanted for anything."

"What's it all about?"

"The Police raided the—" Wagstaff's eyebrows shot up and again he studied Mr. Potter in perplexity — "the Gink Club on a tip that the men who have been doing that series of hotel burglaries were using it as a meeting place. The tip paid off and they got their men."

"But why," Mr. Potter was outraged, "why me?"

"Well, you seem to have been in rather dubious company. Your friend, Trumble, has a police record. Seems to be a confidence man."

"Ridiculous," Mr. Potter said. He added more emphatically, "Ridiculous. I want them released at once."

"Them?"

"My friends, Dr. Trumble and Miss Reed."

Wagstaff's eyes traveled over the small group of people, paused at Opal Reed, turned back to Mr. Potter with the stunned disbelief of one who sees an angora kitten acquire the characteristics of a man-eating tiger. He shook his head. He did some more low-voiced talking.

"All right," he said. "They are being released. Now let's get out of here."

Mr. Potter raised his hat politely to Opal and Dr. Trumble and started out in the wake of Wilbur Wagstaff. As they reached the door a flashbulb went off in his startled face and another and another. Wagstaff, swallowing some angry words, went out to his car and Mr. Potter got in beside him.

"I think," Wagstaff remarked drily as he turned the nose of the car uptown, "we'd better have a talk. Come to the apartment. At your house we won't have any privacy."

This was so unhappily true that Mr. Potter merely nodded in dejection. In front of the apartment building on East Seventy-second Street Wagstaff turned his car over to the doorman and led the way into the huge lobby, with its deep rugs and oil painting softly lighted. The elevator stopped at the eighth floor where there was only one door. Mr. Wagstaff rang and in a few moments a trim maid opened it, as fresh as though it were two-thirty in the afternoon rather than in the morning, and stood back for them to pass.

Even in his flurried state, Mr. Potter realized that Wagstaff had a talent for selecting trim maids. In fact, any woman employee of his was apt to be both shapely and comely. Against his will, Mr. Potter found himself recalling Deborah's malicious comments about the lawyer's personal life, which led him to her comments about Pat and the gangster Rod Miller. He pushed them impatiently out of his mind. Hell hath no fury and all that. There were moments when he found it easy to understand and forgive his cousin's jealousy, suffering as he did from his own.

The pretty maid took their wraps and they went into the big living room where Pat, in a strapless green velvet evening gown sat on a big couch beside Bernard Fullmer, who looked handsomer than ever in a dinner jacket that molded his big shoulders. As the two men entered the room the couple moved apart, Pat made some adjustment to her hair which had become disheveled and Fullmer got to his feet with an easy motion.

Mr. Potter felt as though someone had given his heart a painful wrench. He longed to kick Fullmer across the room but it would make no real difference. Fullmer or no Fullmer, Pat would never look at him.

She waved her hand. "Hi, Jailbird!" she greeted him, her eyes dancing with amusement. "I kept Bernard here by main force to hear all the scandal. And that, let me tell you, is no mean achievement."

Had Pat kept him or had Fullmer remained to find out about the discovery of the girl's body? Mr. Potter longed to say, "Where were you at seven o'clock tonight?" It would be interesting to know what kind of alibi Fullmer would produce.

"Bring some scotch to my study," Mr. Wagstaff instructed the pretty maid.

"No, you don't." Pat was firm. "You stay

right here, both of you. I want to know what Hiram did to get himself a ride in Black Maria."

"Don't be absurd," Wagstaff told his daughter. "Hiram is my client. This is business, dear."

She laughed at him and slipped her hand caressingly under his arm. Wagstaff's face softened, melted. He had always been wax in his daughter's hands. He looked at her now with pride and devotion. A great deal of devotion was necessary for him to consent to her engagement to a man who was hostile to most of his political ideas.

"Come on, Hiram," Pat said cajolingly. "Tell all."

Fullmer gave him his pleasant smile. "You haven't a chance against Pat. But if you're going to spill secrets, perhaps I'd better leave."

"Over my dead body," Pat assured him. "Come on, Hiram – give. What were the exciting events leading up to you being caught in a raid on the –" she laughed – "the Gink Club?"

"It was because of the girl," Mr. Potter said. "I'd like to tell you about it, as a matter of fact, because I don't know what ought to be done. And something has to be done." He had moved slightly so that he could watch Fullmer's expression.

"That girl I got released?" Wagstaff asked. Again he looked at Mr. Potter in perplexity.

"Oh, no! I mean the poor girl who was killed tonight, the one who fell from that Fourth Avenue building into our garden."

Mr. Potter would have been willing to swear that Fullmer revealed nothing beyond the proper sympathy. Certainly he did not look as though guilty knowledge had ever touched him.

"That was a terrible business," he said, meeting Mr. Potter's scrutiny with a bland expression.

"Such a grim thing to happen," Pat added, her warm voice filled with pity. "And they said over the radio that she had been horribly — smashed."

Mr. Potter winced and Wagstaff said, "You take these things too personally, Hiram, too much to heart. In a city as big as this, there are bound to be any number of freak deaths. You can't shoulder the problem of all of them. I know it's worse when, literally, it comes home to you as that did. Still, she was a stranger. Apparently no one saw her fall or knows who she was. According to the radio report, the police have no line on her identity, though they'll probably be able to find out in the morning."

"But she wasn't a stranger. That is," Mr.

Potter said, "I know who she was." For the first time in his life he found himself the center of a group, holding them in enthralled interest. "Her name was Jennie Newcomb." Again he watched Fullmer but the latter's eyes were limpid, he betrayed nothing but a surprised interest.

Mr. Potter told about slipping into the park for a few moments of fresh air and about the girl who had followed him in and fallen into conversation.

"She told me her name and that she had an appointment with someone." He went on to repeat the girl's story about her job and the boss who was being blackmailed. "And she followed me into the park because she mistook me for some other man. I'm afraid it was a man from my own house, because, you see, the park key is missing."

The silence was frozen. Then Pat said flatly, "But that is impossible. You just haven't looked hard enough for it."

"No," Mr. Potter spoke quietly. "You see I noticed Thomas's expression when he got a look at her face. Thomas knew her."

"Thomas!" Wagstaff ejaculated. "Your cousin? But, good God, Hiram." He pushed himself out of his chair and splashed scotch into his glass, so much scotch that Mr. Potter's eyes widened.

Fullmer frowned. "I'm not clear about this," he said in the tone of a man who expects always to be clear about things. "Are you suggesting that your cousin was the girl's employer?"

"I'm suggesting he was the blackmailer," Mr. Potter said. "No one knows yet who employed Jennie Newcomb."

"Nonsense," Wagstaff said. "Someone must know. People who worked in the girl's office. An employment agency. A friend. Her family. Her boss will come forward when she fails to turn up at work."

"Unless," Mr. Potter said, "he is reluctant to attract attention to himself. A man being blackmailed might easily be reticent about publicity."

"Who do you think killed her?" Fullmer asked curiously. "The boss or the blackmailer?"

"The boss," Mr. Potter said promptly. "I'm guessing now but I suspect she told him she had overheard the conversation and he arranged to meet her and silenced her."

Pat had been watching him, her head a little on one side, smiling to herself. "You know, Hiram, you are really rather sweet. Sometimes I wonder how a lamb like you has ever survived in the midst of that Burkett wolf pack."

Mr. Potter did not respond to her smile. Lamb, she said, which could be rather endearing; but what she meant was a sheep, which conjured up only invincible stupidity.

"Why didn't you tell the police you knew the girl's name?" she asked curiously.

"Because Thomas lied when he said he did not know her. I thought it might be advisable to find out what he is up to before I say anything."

"Personally," Pat said coolly, "I regard Thomas Burkett strictly as something that lives on the under side of stones. Crawly. His nasty little-boy ways!"

Wagstaff finished his drink in one long swallow. "Thomas is not one of my favorite people either. When I read your mother's will this afternoon there was an atmosphere, a distinctly uncomfortable feeling – the Burketts are not fond of you, Hiram."

"That," Pat said, "is the understatement of the week. There's nothing too low for them to do to get that money away from you."

"Keep out of this, Pat," her father said. The hour was late and he was exhausted. "Just the same, Hiram, Pat is right up to a point. If the Burketts could get you into trouble they'd do it without hesitation. You'd be wise to leave this whole matter up to me. Let me do any talking to Thomas that is necessary. And when it is necessary. With an unscrupulous fellow like that, there is nothing to gain and a lot to lose by letting him know you talked to the girl, that you know who she was, that you have any suspicions about him."

The lawyer had dropped into one of the low, modernistic chairs Pat loved and, with his short legs sticking straight out, his head tilted back so he could see their faces, he was at a physical disadvantage. Mr. Potter realized that Wagstaff, too, was watching Fullmer intently.

"After all," the older man went on urgently, "you just had a chance meeting with the girl. You don't know anything about her. Get yourself involved in this unsavory business and you'll regret it."

Fullmer attempted to smile but it didn't quite come off. "We all will regret it," he said. "I certainly hope you won't mention that missing key to the police unless it is absolutely necessary. Otherwise, every one of us who was in the house is apt to be involved in an extremely ugly situation. I don't like to be egotistical but I can't afford that, you know. Without being vain, I think I can say that I stand for something that is needed in the country at this time. Scandal would be fatal. I can't have scandal, Potter."

Pat turned to him, a little spasm of alarm on her face. Then she looked at Mr. Potter in appeal. "You won't do anything impulsive, will

72

you? You can't hurt Bernard for the sake of a girl no one knows."

Mr. Potter did not answer immediately. Love did queer things to people; it was warping Pat's fine sense of justice.

"There's one thing you haven't considered, Hiram," Wagstaff said. "You've been thinking the girl must have met a man from your house because the key has been mislaid. And if the man wasn't Thomas, it would have to be either Fullmer or myself. Which, if I may say so, is preposterous. But what about that couple you were with tonight when you were caught in the raid?"

Mr. Potter told him all he knew of Opal Reed and Dr. Trumble, that the former had been Jennie's roommate and the latter was Opal's boy friend who had known Jennie in her home town.

"The reason I ask," Wagstaff said, "is that I figure you have been on the wrong tack about these people all along the line. That fellow Trumble, for instance. He's a confidence man. His specialty is trimming racketeers because they don't make a habit of calling on the police for redress. Usually he gets away with it. But now and then he makes a mistake about his victim and he is caught. If the girl who died was mixed up with people from the criminal classes, there might be half a dozen reasons for getting rid of her that had no possible connection with Thomas."

Fullmer brightened. "That sounds plausible. Anyhow, I know Potter won't rush into things. He has too much good sense." He glanced at his watch. "I must be off. Work is piling up in the office and I need some rest before I tackle it."

Mr. Potter wished that just once Fullmer would display some human weaknesses. The man was too good to be true. He would leave his delectable, adoring Pat in order to get seven hours of tranquil sleep so that he could start his orderly day at the peak of his form. And every hour of the day would be carefully planned so that he would advance step by step toward his goal.

"Oh, darling," Pat said in protest. Then she strolled out of the room with him. There was a murmur of voices in the hallway, a significant pause and then the outer door closed.

Mr. Potter did not want to see Pat with Fullmer's kiss on her mouth and he said good night hastily. Wagstaff hauled himself stiffly out of the chair and followed his guest into the hall.

The older man was feeling his drink. "Look here, Hiram, don't take any steps without consulting me. Publicity right now would ruin

Fullmer and just about break Pat's heart. I won't have my girl hurt."

"But someone's girl has been hurt," Mr. Potter was surprised to hear himself say stubbornly.

"Well, give me a ring in the morning. If Thomas should be involved in any way with this girl, or if he has any knowledge of it, I want you to watch your step. He's unsavory. He could turn nasty. You stand between him and a lot of money, you know."

Mr. Potter knew. As he walked briskly down the street he thought of the rejoicing among the Burketts if he were to be removed permanently. The idea did not distress him. And nothing Wagstaff had said altered his determination to find out what Thomas knew. Thomas held the key to Jennie's murder. His knowledge had been stamped unmistakably on his face for a fleeting moment.

When he had reached the East River Mr. Potter stared unseeingly at the water and lights beyond. Then he turned back, thinking about Wagstaff's warning and Wagstaff's half-glass of scotch. It had not been a bad idea.

He went into a bar and ordered a double whisky. As the fiery liquid went down his throat he began to forget Jennie crashing against the fountain. After a second double whisky Pat's infatuation for Fullmer lost its sharp pain. Under the stimulus of a third, he began to build up a fine truculence toward Thomas.

The more he thought about Thomas the less he thought of Wagstaff's advice. The thing to do was to tackle his cousin at once, force the truth from him. The only difficulty was that his legs gave way when he tried to get off the bar stool.

The weary bartender helped him into a cab. When he reached the house the driver helped him to get out. From a parked car a young man emerged with a camera.

"Mr. Hiram Potter?"

Mr. Potter, clinging to the cabby, blinked owlishly. The young man backed away and a bright light flashed in Mr. Potter's face.

"Who was that girl you were caught with in the raid on the Gink Club, Mr. Potter?...Man, has he a load on! Hey, prop him up until I get another."

The cabby obliged.

"You are disturbing the peace," said a familiar and obnoxious voice, the voice of O'Toole, the radio car patrolman. "You — well, it's Mr. Potter." For a moment the officer obviously toyed with the delightful idea of arresting him and then, with a struggle, he took his arm and half led, half dragged him up the steps and

76

put a massive thumb on the bell.

After some delay, Thomas opened the door. "What the hell—" he began and then, as he looked from O'Toole to the sagging Mr. Potter his eyes widened, his jaw dropped.

O'Toole incautiously let go and Mr. Potter staggered against the door, hanging on to the knob.

"Keep him quiet," the officer said. "Next time he disturbs the peace I'll lock him up."

He went down the steps and Thomas, disentangling Mr. Potter from his grasp on the knob, managed to shut the door, closing out the entranced news man. Deborah came running down the stairs, her eyes glittering.

"Drunk," she cried. "And disorderly. And caught in a raid. And now brought home in this disgusting condition. And reporters calling here all evening. Aren't you ashamed of yourself? The night your mother is buried you bring dishonor on this house. I've never been so humiliated in my life."

Mr. Potter straightened, his eyes opened. "Shut up," he said distinctly.

"Look here," Thomas began, "what the hell's got into you?"

"Not a word," Mr. Potter shouted. "And after this, don't take my car. And I'll get drunk when I want to. I like getting drunk. And I don't like Burketts. I'm going to get rid of all Burketts. And I'm starting with you, Thomas."

Mr. Potter took hold of the banister with both hands and faced Thomas who, in striped pajamas, seemed to be revolving like a barber's pole. "Why didn't you admit you knew that girl? Where did you go tonight? Whom did you see?"

Thomas's expression changed. His eyes were alert and wary. "You're drunk. You don't know what you are talking about."

"Yes, I do. Who killed her, Thomas? Who killed her?"

The jangle of the telephone brought him up short. Thomas started toward it. "I'll take it," Mr. Potter said. He lifted the telephone. "Hello...Hello..." At the other end of the line he could hear someone breathing. Then the connection was broken off.

He pulled himself up, step by step, toiling to the top of the stairs. On the landing he turned to look down at his cousins. "Tomorrow you are going to tell the truth, Thomas, if I have to choke it out of you. Fair warning."

As he closed his bedroom door the telephone began to ring again.

Chapter 6

Without attempting the complicated maneuvers of undressing, Mr. Potter fell on his bed, which behaved in a peculiar way, rocking from side to side so violently that he had to hold on by main strength to keep from being pitched off on the floor. At some dim point the rocking subsided and Mr. Potter dropped as deeply into unconsciousness as though he had been slugged.

Coming back to life was a slow and painful process. Someone was shaking his shoulder, which jarred his head. This set up a chain reaction in Mr. Potter's system that nearly finished him. His head banged with a ferocity he found unbearable, his stomach pitched as his head had done the night before. He tried to open his eyes and the stab of light, even in the dim back bedroom, was almost more than he could bear. In other words Mr. Potter had the grandfather of all hangovers.

He shut his eyes again and settled back cautiously on his pillow. But the shaking of his shoulder continued.

"Don't do that," he protested.

"Mr. Potter—"

Once more he performed the disagreeable act of opening his eyes. When he could focus he saw Tito standing beside the bed, holding a glass that contained a nauseating looking mixture. Mr. Potter shuddered and shut his eyes again.

"Mr. Potter!" This time an arm went under his head, lifted it. "Drink this," Tito said. "You'll feel better."

Obediently, Mr. Potter drank, considered, and decided in relief that his system had no violent objection to the concoction. He could even keep his eyes open.

"I'll bring you some aspirin." Tito went into the bathroom and came back with a glass of water and a bottle of tablets. Mr. Potter swallowed a couple and sipped the water.

"It's almost three o'clock," Tito said when he thought Mr. Potter could comprehend simple words.

"Day or night?"

"Day. When your stomach settles a bit I'll bring you some black coffee."

"I don't want—"

"Mrs. Burkett is waiting to speak to you," Tito said.

"Then you'd better bring the coffee." Holding his head as still as possible, Mr. Potter managed to sit up. He stared dismally at the carpet, a gloomy affair with dark green roses, which he had always hated. What had got into him? Behind him was last night's scandal. Ahead of him was Prudence Burkett. There was no light anywhere. His head sank into his hands. He would have to dress and go down to hear what Aunt Prudence had to say, a meek, chastened and shamed man. And yet, actually, he felt neither meek, chastened nor shamed.

Tito stood back, an expression of alarm on his broad, kindly face. "Mr. Potter, you feel all right?"

Mr. Potter felt terrible. He said so. "But I settled Thomas's hash last night." He was so enlivened by this memory that he decided to get dressed.

This proved to be a slower process than usual but Mr. Potter loved to take his time. He lingered in his shower. He had difficulty in shaving and looked mildly disreputable when he finished, somewhat as though he had had an encounter with an unfriendly cat, a fact he attributed to the tremor of his hands.

He studied himself in the mirror, a carefully dressed young man, with blond hair as sleek and shining as a mirror and an inoffensive face, marred now by bloodshot eyes and scratched cheeks. The face, he told himself, of a man who has been around. On the whole, he was not displeased with his appearance.

Little by little, he became aware of voices, of a sound like that of continually slamming doors. Tito came up with a pot of black coffee and a pile of newspapers.

"What is all that racket?"

"The men from the funeral parlor are collecting their chairs," Tito said in a voice of doom. He set down the tray as though it were the last breakfast of the condemned and spread out the newspapers so Mr. Potter could get the full impact of the front page. Mr. Potter looked, shut his eyes hoping it would go away, and looked again.

There was his own face, trapped and startled; he sagged against a grinning cabby. In the background stood a grim and inexorable O'Toole. The trouble with Mr. Potter was not that he looked villainous; not even, that he looked debauched. He looked ridiculous.

"The telephone," Tito said gloomily, "has been ringing all day and the reporters have been here. With photographers."

Mr. Potter was too crushed to reply, but slowly he began to grow angry. He was becoming weary of being a laughing stock, "Hiram out of Amanda." He was thoroughly tired of the nonentity he had become during Amanda's reign. He was sick of the parasitic Burketts. *In vino veritas.* In his drunken state the night before, he had spoken the truth. He was going to free himself of the people he loathed, of the way of life he detested, of the habits ingrained by years of passive acceptance. More than that, he was going to put up a fight for the girl he loved. He might not have Fullmer's charm but at least he would never dim her gaiety, chill her warmth, strip her of her confidence, try to mold her into an alien pattern.

He went into the front bedroom that had been his mother's and his eye searched for the black sedan. It was gone. In spite of what he had said the night before, Thomas had taken it again. From around the corner of the Players sauntered Adam Faber, his white head hatless, walking in meditative isolation.

Back in his room Mr. Potter read the papers. Hiram Potter, of the wealthy Potter family had been picked up in a raid on the Gink Club a few hours after his mother's funeral. On an inner page were pictures that completed his demoralization. Mr. Potter's companion, Opal

Reed, earned her living as a model and the photographs that had been unearthed by enthusiastic reporters revealed her in so undraped, though comely, a state, that he was overcome with embarrassment. This was awful. This was simply terrible. What would Pat say? He tried to imagine Bernard Fullmer caught in a raid, Bernard Fullmer arrested in the company of an undraped girl. It could not be done. On second thought, however, he was not sure that this was a point in Fullmer's favor.

Nevertheless, some time elapsed before he gathered his forces sufficiently to go on with the papers. Unhappily, the next one was *The Daily Worker.* "Another feeble son of the rich," they called him. They referred to the body that had fallen into the garden behind the Potter house suggested darkly that Mr. Potter knew more than he revealed. Under a better system, they implied, girls would not fall from high buildings.

After three cups of coffee Mr. Potter squared his shoulders and went downstairs. In the main hallway a young man in formal morning dress supervised the removal of the folding chairs. Antonia came out of the drawing room with two big vases of flowers. As usual her enormous breasts seemed to be thrusting themselves through the stout material of her dress. She gave Mr. Potter a quick look as though expecting that his appearance had changed since the day before. She ducked her head warningly toward the drawing room where Mrs. Burkett was sitting with her eyes on the stairway.

Before he could make his escape she called peremptorily, "Hiram!" and he went in to face her.

"Morning Aunt Prudence. Or rather, afternoon, isn't it?"

For a moment she studied him. Then she said coldly, "I am waiting for you to apologize."

"What for?"

The sound, if it had not been too unladylike, could only resemble a snort. "For your preposterous behavior last night, for the humiliation you have brought on us, for that nasty publicity. Models and criminals! To say nothing of coming home in that disgusting drunken state. What the policeman must have thought—"

"Considering the number of times you have called him," Mr. Potter said calmly, "he must be used to coming to this house. Heaven knows, I am sorry about that publicity but I'm not responsible for it."

His aunt was puzzled. For the first time she had an uneasy feeling that she did not understand her nephew, that he might not be as simple to handle as her sister had always found him. Amanda, she remembered, had been firm. She took a firm tone.

"Am I to understand that I'll have to put up with this sort of thing for the rest of my life?"

He sat on the arm of the chair facing her, perched for flight. As though, she thought indignantly, he did not intend to give her time to say what she had to say. She had never noticed before how steady his eyes were.

"It isn't necessary, you know."

It is not easy to build up an emotional scene with someone who remains unruffled but Prudence Burkett did her best. "You quarrel with Thomas; you insult Deborah; you are insolent to me." Her eyes narrowed. "I begin to think I have never known you at all, Hiram."

For a moment something laughed out of his eyes. "That is possible."

Prudence's uneasiness grew. The interview was not advancing in the direction she had planned. If Hiram should not prove to be amenable, what would become of her, of Thomas, of Deborah?

"Remember this," she told him, "you have to give us a home. It's in Amanda's will. I don't know what you have in mind, Hiram, but you won't dare break that will." She added, "I'll appeal to Wilbur Wagstaff, if you do. Pat will find out how you treat your relatives."

"A home, yes," Mr. Potter said. "It is so nominated in the bond." He slid off the arm of the chair. "But mother's will did not indicate what home. It doesn't have to be this one. In fact, it isn't going to be this one."

He took unfair advantage of her temporary speechlessness. "And let's have one thing clear while you are looking for suitable quarters. From now on I want no comment whatever on my behavior."

"Throwing us out!" she choked. "Throwing us out. If Thomas were here—"

"Where is Thomas?"

"I don't know. He must have gone out early this morning. He didn't come down to breakfast. Not a word to me." She sniffed and dabbed at her eyes.

"When he returns, ask him to leave the car key for me, will you? I told him last night I wanted to use the car and it's gone."

Mrs. Burkett opened her mouth to protest, saw the mild blue eyes fixed so steadily on her face, closed it again. They weren't really mild eyes at all, she discovered.

The telephone rang in the library and Mr. Potter went to answer it.

"This is Opal Reed," said the girl at the other end of the wire. She sounded dubious about her reception. "I wanted to thank you for being so nice to us last night. So does Sam. We're both terribly sorry we got you into that awful jam. Just sick about it. And you were so sweet about trying to help us."

"It doesn't matter in the least," Mr. Potter assured her, answering her honest distress rather than her words.

"Oh, it does," she said in her quick, emphatic voice. "Being picked up in that raid and all the publicity in the papers. And you got us out, too. Sam says you are a real gentleman and he wants to shake your hand."

Mr. Potter declared that he was much gratified.

"If you aren't just plain disgusted with us, we'd like to get together for a talk," Opal said. "Can you meet us for a drink somewhere?"

Mr. Potter considered the idea of inviting them to the house on Gramercy Park and abandoned it. "Anywhere but the Gink Club," he said and grinned when he observed that Prudence Burkett had stiffened to attention.

Opal laughed shakily. "Not the Gink Club," she agreed. "I wouldn't bother you except that something's happened. Something queer. Something — wrong."

Something very wrong, Mr. Potter thought, judging by her voice. He asked cautiously, aware of his aunt listening in the background,

"Did you go — ah — did you see—"

Opal drew in her breath and it came out in uneven gusts. "That's what — that—" she broke off, steadied. "Look Mr. Potter, if you are willing to come here to my apartment on Eighth Street we could talk more privately."

Mr. Potter said he would be there in half an hour. As he reentered the drawing room, Mrs. Burkett looked without favor at his bloodshot eyes, his scratched face.

"A wolf," she told him bitterly, "in sheep's clothing."

Mr. Potter beamed. Under those conditions he didn't mind having even Pat regard him as a sheep.

"Where are you going?" she demanded.

"Out," said Mr. Potter.

II

Mr. Potter started for the front door and halted when he heard raised voices from the Petrellas in the basement. Antonia, who had been doing most of the talking, broke off as he came into the room. She eyed Mr. Potter with furtive curiosity.

"What's wrong?" he asked.

"Tito always puts off," she said in exasperation. "The garden looks terrible and now there are pictures of it in the paper because the girl fell there and people will think it was always kept like that. If I've told him once I've told him a dozen times to fix up the hedge that shuts off the alley."

"What's the matter with it?"

Antonia swept Mr. Potter through the house and out through the narrow lower hall into the little garden. There was a brown stain on the side of the fountain and a flower bed that had been trampled by the feet of policemen. Neither of them spoke of it as she led him hastily past.

"Some kids who were sore at Mrs. Burkett for calling the police when they were playing in the park broke through the hedge a while ago. Trying to get even, I guess."

"Tito can work on it in his spare time." After telling her that he would not return for dinner, Mr. Potter went through the break in the hedge. It was typical, he thought, of his position in the house that no one had informed him of the vendetta between his aunt and the children who played in the park.

For a moment he stood in the alley, aware of the ashcans that had been rolled out of the basement of the big office building from which Jennie had fallen to her death. How had it been managed? In the park she might have been taken by surprise and knocked out. But in an almost deserted building at night, she would be suspicious, on her guard. No, he thought, remembering the hallucination in her eyes, she would go obediently where she was told. She had been the most suggestible human being he had ever seen.

But why the office building? That would imply a familiarity with the building, a reasonable assurance that the murderer could get in and out unobserved.

Rain began to fall and Mr. Potter went in through the basement door that opened on the alley. There was no one in the furnace room and he skirted the freight elevator, taking a narrow stairway that led to the first floor. The stair well appeared to go to the top floor of the building but it was unlikely Jennie could have been made to walk so far.

Mr. Potter emerged into the main lobby. Only one elevator of a bank of seven was on the floor and that one was unloading passengers. No one looked toward the back of the lobby although several people stopped at the combination newsstand and cigar counter in front. At night, only one elevator would be in use and the operator would probably be dozing or reading a magazine somewhere in the lobby.

Another elevator came down and discharged

passengers. Mr. Potter noticed that only five were passenger elevators; one was for freight and the one farthest back was a self-service affair with a sign: "PRIVATE – KEEP OUT."

He strolled down to the newsstand and bought some cigarettes. "What is the private elevator for?"

"Penthouse."

"I didn't know there was one."

The news man nodded. "That's New York for you. I've worked in this building for years and didn't know the house was up there until about a year ago when some workmen came to repair the elevator. The house is set so far back it doesn't show, except now and then in summer when you notice the canopies and trees from a high roof. Nice little place. I went up to take a look once. Except for half a dozen people, like watchmen and furnace men, no one in the building seemed to know about it." He winked. "Guy who owns it keeps it for parties and isn't here much of the time."

The fortunate owner of the penthouse, it emerged, was a man named Morland who was now in Europe. He wasn't going to like having the place written up now the girl had fallen from the building, but maybe he had enough influence to keep the existence of his penthouse out of the news. Oh, sure, he answered Mr.

Potter's question, the police knew all about him and they had gone up to investigate. But the girl had not been in the penthouse. Morland had a burglar alarm that would raise the dead and it had not been tampered with.

Kind of parties Morland gave, he'd need to keep on the good side of the police. Orgies, that's what they were. Orgies.

Whatever ideas Mr. Potter might be acquiring, they were discarded at once. Morland was in Paris, the police had reached him there. The description of the girl hadn't meant a thing to him though he admitted he had entertained girls frequently. Only thing was that the one who killed her must have known about the penthouse. Seemed like it must have been the private elevator that was used. They'd found threads from her dress. She'd gone out a window on the twentieth floor and unless she walked she'd gone in the private elevator.

Mr. Potter hovered. Rain began to fall heavily. At a quarter of five the elevators hummed as office workers came down, herding toward the doorway and the rain-swept streets and crowded subways, exclaiming over the storm. Some of the girls brought newspapers to protect their hats and darted out; others waited inside the doors. Mr. Potter watched his opportunity, walked up two flights, rang the bell of the private elevator, stepped inside and went up. He emerged into a narrow hallway with two doors, one of which led outside to the penthouse, the other to the stairs. He pushed the down button on the elevator, got out at the third floor, sent the elevator down and walked down the stairs to the basement and out into the alley. Getting in and out of the building unobserved was simple enough if one knew the ropes, but only a gambler would have taken the chance.

Because there was no point in trying to hail a taxi in the rain, Mr. Potter pulled his hat down, his collar up, and ran for the downtown subway at Twenty-third Street.

At Ninth Street he got out in the basement of Wanamaker's Store, forced his way past wet raincoats and soggy umbrellas up to the street and turned west, looking for Opal Reed's address. The first time he passed it and had to turn back. It seemed like an improbable place for Opal to live, a dark, narrow stairway between a cleaning establishment and an artist-supply shop. There were only three cards: Opal Reed and Jennie Newcomb lived on the second floor.

Opal opened the door at his knock and held out her hand. "Welcome, Mr. Potter. Sam was just wondering if you'd be able to find it."

Sam Trumble put down the newspaper he

had been reading and shook hands warmly. "This guy," he told Opal, "is regular."

The little room into which Opal proudly ushered him was so tiny he wondered how it could hold three people. There was a couch with a cheap, ill-fitting cover, a card-table with two folding chairs, and a worn leather arm-chair. She waved him toward the latter.

"You fix the drinks," she told him.

Mr. Potter blanched. "Not a drink," he said with a shudder.

"I don't know how to ask you to forgive us," Opal said. "Sam and I feel just terrible. Getting you into all that trouble."

"Nonsense," he said briskly.

"Atta boy," Sam said with approval. "Now let Dr. Trumble prescribe for you. What you need — what you're going to have — is a hair of the dog that bit you."

Chapter 7

Drastic as the prescription appeared, it worked. After the first drink Mr. Potter felt that he would live; after the second, he did not even object to living.

He leaned back in the shabby armchair, benevolently disposed toward the world, with a warm fellow feeling for Opal Reed and Sam Trumble. He was the man who had charged to the rescue, the honored guest. All that bothered him was a faint embarrassment over having seen the revealing photographs of Opal, having heard Wagstaff's account of Sam's activities. Neither Opal nor Sam appeared to share this embarrassment. Opal hovered around Mr. Potter as though he were an invalid on the verge of collapse. Sam smiled amiably through his horn-rimmed glasses. As nice a fellow, Mr. Potter thought, as you'd want to meet.

"It was mighty good of you to get us released," Sam said.

"Not at all," mumbled Mr. Potter.

"I suppose," Sam said easily, "your lawyer told you about me."

"Well — that is—"

Sam set his briefcase on the floor and leaned back on the couch, legs stretched out, hands clasped behind his neck. "I'm not trying to make any excuses. Understand? I'm just telling you how it is. I grew up in an orphanage and when I left there everyone who gave me a job acted as though he was doing me a big favor and sweated hell out of me. I was just a kid and I worked my heart out, thinking how big-hearted they were.

"Once when I was at the orphanage in Florida some group took a bunch of us out on a boat, one of those glass-bottomed ones. Ever go on one?"

Mr. Potter nodded.

"Little fish at the top trying to get away from bigger ones below. And those were getting away from still bigger ones. All the way down. So I got to looking around and thinking." Sam took off his glasses, polished them and tapped them against the side of the table to emphasize his points. "Divide people up and you get the ones who prey and the ones who are preyed upon. So I figured I'd get my slice, only I didn't want to go to jail for it. That's why I picked the racketeers. Funny how gullible crooks are. And they can't squeal when they're hurt because they are outside the law."

He looked quickly at Mr. Potter. "So I do all right. As a rule."

"But you are outside the law, too," Mr. Potter pointed out.

"So what?"

"It must be rather lonely."

"You see," Opal broke in. "I keep telling you, Sam. Think what it would be like to settle down. Think of being able to live somewhere for good and not carry around that briefcase with an extra shirt in it in case you have to move on in a hurry. Think of not bothering about being caught."

"How often does that happen?" he demanded.

"It's happening right now," she reminded him.

Sam was on the defensive. "How did I know the guy had an in with the cops?"

Opal explained that Sam had miscalculated and his most recent victim had made a complaint. Sam, at the moment, was dodging the police.

"When you're smart enough to find out you are the sucker," Mr. Potter said, "come to see me and we'll try to work out something."

"And now you've got that settled," Opal said, "I want to talk about Jennie." She began to shake and Sam reached for her, drew her down beside him, took her hands firmly in his.

Early that afternoon Opal and Sam had gone to the morgue to view the body of the girl they believed to be Jennie Newcomb.

When they got inside, Sam had gripped Opal's arm and whispered, "That's Jennie's stepmother. I've got to clear out before she recognizes me." Before she could protest he had gone.

The woman whom he had pointed out was a behemoth, at least six feet tall, broad of shoulder and heavy of build. She had a masculine face with a long, cruel upper lip and small eyes embedded in pouches. She was almost aggressively unattractive. Her face, except for a careless streak of powder, was devoid of makeup; her gray hair was unwaved and hung dankly around her face.

She had asked to see the body of the girl who had fallen from the office building. Opal flung out her hands, pushing away the thing she had seen. At last she swallowed hard and went on. The big woman had turned so white the attendant had grabbed her arm, thinking she was going to faint. Then she had identified Jennie as her stepdaughter. She said she had flown from Hackers Point, Ohio, to view the body.

"She said," Opal set her teeth hard and then went on, "she said she'd been expecting something like that. She said Jennie had been despondent because she had been jilted by someone in New York. She said Jennie had written that she was going to kill herself."

"I don't believe it," Mr. Potter said.

"There's not a word of truth in it," Sam put in. "Jennie didn't know any men, she was a stranger here and she spent all her evenings with Opal or with the two of us." His mouth was not pleasant at all. "What I'd like to know is how much the old harridan was paid for saying that."

For a moment they were all thoughtful and then Opal got up and tied an apron around her slim waist. She was pale but determined.

"I'll get dinner while you two talk." She went into the kitchenette where Mr. Potter could hear a vigorous clatter of kettles.

It was Mr. Potter who spoke first. "So the police are just going to write it off as suicide," he said in a tone of unbelief. "I'll be damned if they are!"

There was a scurry of footsteps, Opal ran out to plant a moist kiss on Mr. Potter's nose. He beamed.

Sam chuckled. "Get on with that dinner," he told Opal who gave him a fleeting hug and went back to the kitchenette. "Where do we start?" he asked Mr. Potter.

"At least I know how Jennie got into the building," Mr. Potter said and he described his explorations of the Fourth Avenue office building.

"Of course," Sam said thoughtfully, "the police have figured that out. But if she didn't go by herself, if she was taken there, it must have been by someone who knew of that self-service elevator; perhaps someone who knew Morland well enough to have gone to one of the parties in the penthouse."

Mr. Potter nodded. That could apply to Thomas who was an enthusiastic party man so long as he did not have to pay for them. He had never heard Thomas mention Morland, though that did not mean anything. Thomas was not exactly forthright in spite of his youthfully confiding manner.

For a moment Mr. Potter thought longingly of Fullmer. What a magnificent feat it would be to show the fellow up as the villain of the piece. He brooded, reluctantly abandoned the idea. Fullmer was a dedicated man; when he attended parties it was in the pure and disinterested hope of meeting people who would further his career. Morland's parties could hardly have come in that category. They were more likely to be in Wagstaff's line of country, provided there were girls enough and a little gambling on the side. Mr. Potter did not pursue the idea; it was not Wagstaff whom he was after. Definitely, he was not on the track of Pat's father.

"Your cousin didn't kill Jennie," Sam said, "and he's about the only one we can eliminate. Whatever he may know, he couldn't have killed her. He was right under your eyes when she fell. But if he knew who she was, he may know a lot more. You've got to get that information out of him, Potter, one way or another. And be careful."

"My lawyer has already warned me that Thomas is dangerous."

"Not dangerous to you, perhaps, but dangerous to himself. A blackmailer — if he is a blackmailer — is asking for it. We don't want him dropping out of a high window. Not, at least, until he has told what he knows or suspects. Who else was at your house? This fellow Fullmer. Your lawyer, Wilbur Wagstaff — is he the stout little pouter pigeon who talked Opal and me out of jail last night?" When Mr. Potter nodded he asked, "Did he know the guy with the penthouse?"

"Morland? I've never heard him say so." Mr. Potter added reluctantly, "My cousin Deborah says Wagstaff is a chaser. Personally, I've never believed anything she says. Still, I realize that we can't overlook anything. If she is right he might have been at one of Morland's parties."

"Is Patricia Wagstaff any relation of his?" Opal asked unexpectedly.

Mr. Potter stiffened. "His daughter."

"Then I know her. That is, I've seen her a lot but not to speak to. She works over at the Settlement House three afternoons a week. I go there quite often. I've got friends there." Opal added with a touch of defiance, "I'm from the slums myself."

"Then they have been maligned," Mr. Potter said gallantly.

Opal, spreading a cloth on the cardtable, let her defiance drop away, half ashamed. "She's the one, isn't she?"

When Mr. Potter made no reply she said, "Miss Wagstaff is your girl friend. I can tell by the way you sound when you mention her."

"No," Mr. Potter said hastily, "she's engaged to marry Fullmer."

Opal started to speak, looked at him thoughtfully and then changed her mind. "What are we going to do about Mrs. Newcomb? Let her get away with it? If you'd seen her there be-

103

side – beside Jennie." Her voice broke. "She didn't seem even sorry. Jennie might have been anyone. A stranger."

While they ate bacon and eggs they sketched out their plans.

"You'd better tackle Mrs. Newcomb," Sam told Mr. Potter. "She knows me and I wouldn't get to first base. But she doesn't know you. Anyhow, you've got the one thing that will make her talk."

When Mr. Potter looked his question, Sam jingled the coins in his pocket. He had known the Newcombs, he said, in Hackers Point, Ohio. The old man owned a garage and had died just a few months earlier. Mrs. Newcomb was his second wife and a tartar. She sold the garage and put all the money into a little bake-shop. Jennie never got a penny of it. Mrs. Newcomb had always been unkind to the kid and she'd have sold her own mother into slavery for money. The miserly kind. Liked to take the money out of the till just to handle it.

Sam leaned forward and removed his glasses. "She's a witch," he said. "One, Mrs. Newcomb always had it in for Jennie because the old man was so fond of her. Two, we know she is lying about Jennie being jilted. Three, someone must have bribed her to come forward with that suicide story in order to get the police off the case.

There was no picture of Jennie in the papers — there couldn't be, judging by what Opal told me — so how did she know?"

"If you are right," Mr. Potter said, "Mrs. Newcomb is in a bad spot. If she came here with that cock-and-bull story about Jennie's suicide, she is covering for the girl's murderer. How long do you think she'll be safe?"

Sam shrugged. "I don't give a damn what happens to her. I tell you she'd sell her soul for coin of the realm. You should see the way she hustled Jennie off to New York when old Newcomb died, so she could get her hands on that garage and turn it into cash."

"Is that why Jennie was so eager to earn a bonus?"

"Probably. She didn't have fifty dollars in the world when she hit town. God knows what would have happened to her if Opal hadn't taken her in."

"How am I to find the woman?" Mr. Potter asked.

"She told them at the morgue," Opal said, "she was staying at the City Hotel for a day."

"That's a good place," Sam pointed out. "A big commercial hotel is so crowded all the time that no one would be likely to notice the people she saw there."

"And how do I persuade her to tell the truth?"

"Pull out your checkbook," Sam said, "and stand back so you won't be killed in the rush."

It sounded easy.

II

Mr. Potter got off the Sixth Avenue bus at Forty-second Street, back of the library, and walked over to Broadway. It was too late for movie-goers, too early for the theaters to close; and the rain, now changing to sleet, made that improbable street comparatively empty, save for buses, cruising taxis, and the peculiar Broadway species that comes out after dark, regardless of the weather.

Mr. Potter went past the Astor Hotel, headed north and in a few blocks turned west. You couldn't miss the enormous sign of the City Hotel. Inside, Mr. Potter looked around the huge, sparsely furnished lobby. However deserted the streets might be, the lobby was thronged with impatient men and women waiting for someone, waiting for the rain to stop, just waiting. There were the drifters, the homeless and the rootless; there were minor actors who were "resting," pickpockets, the floating scum of Times Square.

He pushed his way through the crowd to the

106

desk where he was given the number of Mrs. Newcomb's room. From a telephone on the desk he called the number. A twangy midwestern voice answered.

"Mrs. Newcomb?"

"This is Mrs. Newcomb."

"May I see you for a few minutes?"

"No more reporters," she said crisply. "I've said all I have to say."

"I'm not a reporter."

"Well, what do you want?"

"I'm — a friend of Jennie's."

In the ensuing pause he could hear the sound of her breathing. "All right," she said at last. "But only for fifteen minutes, mind. I'm worn out from traveling and I've got to get some sleep."

Mr. Potter shoved his way into a crowded elevator, edged his way off on the seventh floor and went past the floor clerk who was talking to one of the chamber maids and did not even glance at him. Sam had been right, he thought. No one would be noticed in a hotel like this.

The woman who opened the door in answer to his knock was enormous. Even Sam's description had not prepared him for her sheer size. "She punished first," Jennie had said. Mrs. Newcomb would enjoy punishing. She looked Mr. Potter over as though he were a chicken she were selecting for dinner. He would not have been altogether surprised if one of the big hands had reached out and prodded his breast bone.

Reluctantly she stood aside to let him enter the uninviting room, pointed out an uncomfortable chair and sat on the edge of the bed, which sagged ominously under her weight. The room was on a court and filled with the magnified noise of a brass band on the first floor whose sounds echoed and re-echoed in the narrow shaft.

"Well?" she said. It was hardly the tone of a grieving mother who had just looked upon the broken body of her daughter. Hardly the tone one uses to a friend of the dead.

"I came to see you," Mr. Potter said, "because I wanted to talk to you about Jennie."

She shook her head. "It's an awful thing. An awful thing. Poor girl." The small hard eyes peered from their pouches. "Did you know her well?"

"I met her only once."

Whatever she had expected, this was not it. Mrs. Newcomb betrayed her surprise and something very like relief. She settled herself more firmly. "What's your name?"

"Potter. Jennie fell into the garden between my house and the office building."

The woman who had been Jennie's step-mother shivered convulsively. For a moment she was touched by some of the horror of that terrible fall. It struck Mr. Potter that, being essentially an unimaginative woman, she had not pictured the manner of the girl's death clearly before.

"I understand," he said, "that you think her death was suicide."

Mrs. Newcomb's voice was sharp. "Of course it was suicide! As I told the police, she wrote me herself that she intended to do it."

"But there was no man, Mrs. Newcomb. Jennie's roommate tells me she didn't know any men in New York — except for her employer."

"That model! I saw pictures of her in the papers. A brazen piece, posing nude before a lot of men. Jennie never dared tell me how she earned her living."

"Still it is fortunate," Mr. Potter said smoothly, "Miss Reed could earn a living. Otherwise, Jennie would have been homeless as well as penniless."

The big woman stirred. "What are you trying to prove, Mister?"

"Who was Jennie's employer, Mrs. Newcomb?"

The big hands clenched slowly, crushing the bed clothes. "I don't know."

"Did you keep Jennie's letter? The one in which she said she had been jilted?"

She hesitated. She was not a quick thinker. "I don't have it with me. As you barely knew her, I can't see what business this is of yours, why you can't let her rest in peace."

"I think she was murdered," Mr. Potter said quietly. "And people can't be allowed to do that, if we are to keep civilized."

"If that naked model said so, she'd better watch her step." The big woman spoke harshly and then was aware herself that her strident tone was excessive in reply to this quiet man, this disturbingly quiet man.

His tone was so mild that for a moment she did not take in the meaning of his words. "What made you think it was Jennie who had been killed? Who told you about it, Mrs. Newcomb?"

Her eyes wavered. "I saw the pictures in the paper."

"There were no pictures of her in the papers."

Mrs. Newcomb heaved her great body off the bed. "Call me a liar, will you?" Again the big hands clenched in a ruthless, crushing movement. "You want to be careful who you go calling a liar, Mr. Potter." Her eyes opened wide with as poorly staged an effect of surprise as Mr. Potter had ever seen. "Potter! Why that's the name Jennie mentioned, the man who jilted her."

Aside from his more active months in the army Mr. Potter had never looked upon active evil. He stared at her for a moment in almost unbelieving horror. Her long upper lip lifted in a smile that did not touch her eyes.

"I don't want to make anyone trouble. Live and let live. That's my motto. Anyhow, Jennie is gone and we can't bring her back. But I don't like snoopy, trouble-making little squirts. Try to make me trouble and I'll have to tell the police the name of the man who jilted Jennie. Hiram Potter, that's who it was."

"How did you know that my name is Hiram?"

For a moment her eyes were curiously fixed. "Jennie wrote it to me," she said in a tone of triumph. "She told me, Mr. Two-timing Potter."

It occurred to Mr. Potter that he had completely overlooked the one factor Sam had believed would bring the woman to terms. He reached in his pocket and pulled out a checkbook. "I will give you my personal check for one thousand dollars if you will tell me how you knew Jennie was dead."

She stood quite still, her eyes fixed on the checkbook, one big hand curving as though she held the money in her hand. The struggle in her was like pain.

"A thousand dollars," she said at length. "Why I could—" She stopped. Again he heard the heavy asthmatic breathing he had noticed over the telephone.

"Five thousand," he said. "But that is my final price."

"Five thousand."

Mr. Potter, watching her face, had the curious illusion that for a moment he saw piles of silver dollars, gleaming dollars, rolling through her hands. Then that odd impression faded.

"Why?" she asked.

"Because I can't let a murderer go free." He flipped open the checkbook, turned it carelessly so that she could read the amount of the balance.

Again the breathing was loud in the room. Once she started to speak, her big hand curving toward him, toward the checkbook, toward those glittering, illusory dollars. Then with an effort at control that left her shaking, she dropped her hand.

"Get out of here," she said.

"You are being stupid, you know," Mr. Potter said almost lazily as he replaced his checkbook. "A murderer has nothing to lose by a second crime. I advise you to tell the police what you know. Otherwise I'd hate to be in your shoes."

"I can take care of myself," she said. "You aren't scaring me none." But he was, he was scaring her horribly.

"That's rather a pity," he said. "Sure you won't change your mind?"

"I told you once before. I tell you for the last time: Jennie – killed – herself."

He shrugged and let himself quietly out of the room.

From a telephone booth in the lobby he called Opal to report on his interview. She was furious, her voice muffled as she tried to talk to him and to Sam at the same time. Then the latter came on the wire.

"At least," Sam said in a tone of satisfaction, "we know she must be sure of a lot of money if she turned down your offer. I wonder what she'll do now."

Mr. Potter was looking through the glass door of the booth. "She's gone to collect," he said. "I'm going to follow her."

But the crowd in the lobby defeated him. By the time he reached the street Mrs. Newcomb was out of sight.

Chapter 8

When Mr. Potter reached Gramercy Park that night he saw the black sedan had been returned. He went up the steps, shaping in his mind the comments he was going to make to Thomas.

Mrs. Burkett darted out of the drawing room as he opened the front door. Her face fell. "I thought you were Thomas." She lifted her voice. "Deborah, it's only Hiram."

"Thomas must be home," Mr. Potter said. "The car is here."

"We don't know where Thomas is." She drew him back into the drawing room where she had been seated before a dying fire. Deborah looked up from her eternal game of canfield at the small table near the long windows.

"Mother is nearly frantic," she said. "Thomas went out — well, actually, we don't know when he went. He might even have gone out last night. Someone telephoned just after you went upstairs. Thomas answered but he just said yes and okay so I don't know who it was. Anyhow, he wasn't here for breakfast and there hasn't been a word from him all day."

"Something has happened," Mrs. Burkett declared in the voice of Cassandra. "I know something has happened. Thomas would never let me worry like this. I intend to call the police."

"I keep telling her he'd hate that," Deborah said. "It will make him feel like a fool."

Mr. Potter agreed. "Better let it go until morning, Aunt Prudence. After all, it's not eleven o'clock yet. Early. The police won't pay much attention to a call like that. Why don't you go to bed and get some rest?"

"Heaven knows I need rest," his aunt snapped. "What with the telephone going like mad last night and those reporters besieging us after you got involved in that disgusting raid, and then coming home drunk, dragged in by a policeman — I hardly closed my eyes all night. And," she added in a belated afterthought, "after the strain and sorrow of my sister's funeral. Though I must say she deserved to have someone grieve for her, with her only son actually celebrating with a naked model."

Mr. Potter took a long breath. "Deborah, haven't you a sleeping pill you can give your mother?"

Deborah took her upstairs and Mr. Potter built up the fire until the crackling logs brought brightness and warmth to the room, and turned on the radio, switching to WQXR. He listened to William Kappell floating through the improbable pyrotechnics of Liszt's Mephisto Waltz. Not great music, maybe, but there is always pleasure, as Lemaître pointed out, in seeing anything done perfectly.

Deborah came down the stairs, abandoned the cardtable, and sat beside Mr. Potter. "Mother is crying herself to sleep. She is nearly out of her head with worry."

"But why? After all," he looked at his watch, "eleven-thirty isn't a fatal hour for a party man like Thomas."

"Mother says she doesn't think he came home at all last night. Antonia told her his bed hadn't been touched. No one has seen him since you quarreled with him."

Mr. Potter's lips puckered in a faint whistle. "What do you think he's up to?"

"I don't know."

"By the way, Deborah, did you ever hear of a man named Morland? He owns a penthouse at the office building back of us."

"Morland? The name sounds familiar. Oh!" Deborah's face cleared. "Yes, Thomas went to one of his parties. Quite a while ago. I remember he was very amused about something."

"Recently?"

"No – in the fall, I think. Just before he bought his moving picture camera and screen and set up the little theater in the basement." She yawned. "It's really inconsiderate of Thomas to stay away without letting mother know. She fusses so about him."

"At least, he brought back the car. He'll probably show up before long."

But Thomas Burkett did not come home that night. In the morning Mrs. Burkett called the police. Within a few minutes the familiar radio car drew up in front of the house and Tito admitted O'Toole. By this time, Mrs. Burkett was enjoying an attack of hysterics that equalled anything Deborah had been able to achieve, so Mr. Potter had to face his *bête noir*.

"Good morning, officer," he said briskly. "Personally, I think my aunt is all upset over nothing."

O'Toole's good-looking face was marred by the scowl which Mr. Potter always evoked. "Usually is," he commented.

"The point is that her son, my cousin Thomas, went out early yesterday morning – actually, no one has seen him since the night before – and he hasn't come back. Not to the house, in any case. He took my car and returned it

117

some time yesterday."

Mr. Potter moved so that the light fell full on his face and O'Toole studied with interest the fading scratches caused by yesterday's unsteady hand when he shaved.

"He'll probably turn up on his own. Still, we'll check. Do you have a picture of him?"

"Aunt Prudence has a whole album of pictures of him." Mr. Potter rang for Tito and asked him to find the photograph album.

"Where does he work?"

"He doesn't have any occupation," Mr. Potter said.

"Independent income?"

"Well, an allowance. Hardly enough to make him independent, but of course he lives here."

Deborah ran down the stairs ahead of Tito, the album clasped in her arms. She helped O'Toole select a picture that showed Thomas full face and one of his profile. It was too much to expect that she would pass up a dramatic opportunity and Mr. Potter watched helplessly, knowing that the outburst was bound to come.

She looked at him. "I hope you're ashamed now of the way you treated him! If anything happens, I hope you'll be ashamed!"

She ran back upstairs and Mr. Potter turned to see the alert, speculative look on O'Toole's face. It occurred to him that it would be as well if nothing untoward happened to Thomas.

"He the guy who let you in the house night before last?" asked O'Toole.

Mr. Potter nodded, recalling, with a sinking heart, his shouts and threats, which had been overheard not only by the officer but probably by the camera man who had been waiting outside and the cabby who had appeared to enjoy the whole business.

O'Toole turned on his heel and went down the back stairs to the Petrellas' room. Unashamed, Mr. Potter hung over the railing, eavesdropping, while O'Toole questioned Tito. No, Tito didn't know what had happened to Thomas Burkett and, what was more, he didn't care. Nasty piece of work, sneaky sort of fellow, always taking advantage of Mr. Potter's good nature and Mr. Potter letting him get away with it. Never had he been so glad in his life, Tito went on, warming to his task, as when Mr. Potter had told him yesterday that he had settled Thomas's hash.

"Well," O'Toole said happily. "Well, well." He asked, "When did Mr. Potter get those scratches on his face? He didn't have them when I let him in the house."

II

The police reported several times during the day. No one answering to Thomas's description had turned up in hospitals, street accidents or at the morgue. Thomas himself did not call. Early in the afternoon, Patricia Wagstaff telephoned and asked Mr. Potter to accompany her to a political rally that evening where Bernard Fullmer was to speak. Mr. Potter boldly suggested dinner and Pat agreed.

By evening, when he was dressing to take Pat to dinner and to the rally, even Mr. Potter was becoming perplexed by Thomas's continued absence. On impulse he went up to the third floor where the Burketts had their bedrooms, Mrs. Burkett and Deborah in the front and back bedrooms, Thomas in the middle room.

Thomas's bed had certainly not been slept in. Mr. Potter opened the closet door and was taken aback by the extent of his cousin's wardrobe, by the number of tailormade suits, the handmade shoes neatly treed, the rack of expensive neckwear. He went through the bureau drawers, turning over in mounting surprise the monogramed shirts, observing the number and quality of the stickpins, cufflinks, cigarette cases and lighters. Thomas did himself very well indeed.

He went back to the closet and saw that all his luggage was stacked on the shelves. Wherever he was, he had not planned to go away.

After a moment's hesitation, with some reluctance and distaste, Mr. Potter looked through the desk. There were receipted bills for large amounts but apparently no outstanding debts. There was no personal correspondence whatever. But, tucked into a leather box under a pile of stationery there was a small address book lying on top of a thick stack of money, which totalled twenty-five hundred dollars.

Mr. Potter put back the money and slipped the address book into his pocket. Amanda's allowance, Thomas's only visible source of income, could never, by any stretch of the imagination, have added up to a reserve of this size. Thomas had never gone away, of his own free will, leaving the cash behind him.

When Mr. Potter came down the stairs, deep in thought, he found Mrs. Burkett, red eyed, huddled over a gloomy fire. Deborah sat at her endless game of canfield. Mr. Potter looked at the two women. How dismal they made the drawing room. How dismal they made the house. As damp as the tear-stained cheeks that left watermarks on Elizabeth Barrett Browning's sonnets. He wondered what it would be like to have Pat in the house. Open windows and fresh breezes and sunshine, he answered himself immediately. Laughter instead of tears. Gaiety instead of gloom.

"Well," he said with forced cheerfulness, "I'm off."

"I suppose you realize," Deborah said spitefully, "the only reason you are taking Pat Wagstaff to dinner is because Bernard doesn't eat before making a speech and she has to have some man."

"Oh, of course," Mr. Potter agreed. "See you later."

He let himself out of the house with a feeling of liberation and slid under the wheel of the sedan. He groped in his pocket for the key and then noticed in surprise that Thomas had left it in the switch. Of all the careless things to do!

The sedan moved smoothly around the park and up Lexington Avenue. Mr. Potter let down the window and felt the air on his face. Just for an hour, he thought, it was permissible to forget Jennie. This was his evening alone with Pat and he intended to make the most of it.

She was waiting when he arrived, warm and glowing in a soft yellow dinner dress with discreet lines and long sleeves, doubtless chosen with an eye to Fullmer's constituents. She slipped her arm under his and led him into her father's small study, a dark room with a low lamp on the desk, old paintings well lighted, and a small fire burning in the grate.

Wagstaff snapped off the light on his desk when they came in and the pretty maid followed with a tray of cocktails.

"Well, Hiram," Wagstaff said, "what's happening to your mystery?"

"Which mystery?" Mr. Potter asked. "Jennie or Thomas?"

"Thomas?" Wagstaff repeated blankly.

Mr. Potter sighed. "It's probably in the evening papers by now. I haven't dared to look. Thomas seems to have vanished."

"Good," Pat declared with heartfelt approval. "I've been longing for years to have Thomas vanish. Something about that boyish manner of his really makes me ill."

"Stop it, Pat," her father said. "This is serious. What do you think happened to him, Hiram?"

"I haven't any idea. Frankly, I'm like Pat. The more completely Thomas vanishes the better I'd like it. Only—"

"Well?"

"There's something wrong," Mr. Potter said. "I don't believe Thomas is staying away deliberately. In fact, I'm certain of it."

"Why?"

"Because he left twenty-five hundred dollars

in a drawer of his desk."

"And where," Pat scoffed, "would Thomas get that kind of money?"

Wagstaff finished his drink and poured another. The time came, Mr. Potter thought, when a man aged fast. For years the lawyer had appeared not to change at all, but now he was old. Not up to handling the kind of problems that Mr. Potter was facing. He was past it. Mr. Potter found that, on the whole, he was pleased to be on his own.

Wagstaff gave him a long, troubled look. "You know," he suggested at length, "I don't think I'd go around broadcasting my personal opinion of Thomas if I were you. I don't like this. He might just possibly have landed himself in a nasty mess." He poured himself a third cocktail, and Mr. Potter wondered whether he had ever before seen the lawyer dispose of drinks so rapidly.

"Aunt Prudence called the police but I don't think they are taking Thomas's disappearance too seriously. She calls them about something half a dozen times a week, from all I can make out."

"Do they know about that cache of money?"

Mr. Potter shook his head. "I didn't discover it until just before I left the house this evening."

"What did you do with it?"

Mr. Potter was surprised. "Left it where I found it, of course."

Pat laughed suddenly. "Hiram, in some ways you are adorable."

"How is your other mystery coming along?" Wagstaff asked, cheering up as he always did when Pat revealed some interest in Hiram. Perhaps the very fact he had Wagstaff's full approval made him less interesting to Pat.

"I'm forgetting it for this one evening," he said. "When Pat has dinner with me, that's an occasion."

Wagstaff looked at the two young people. "So far as I am concerned," he said drily, "it's an occasion that could be a lot more frequent than it is."

Pat rubbed her cheek against his hair. "Old sour puss! Some day you'll appreciate Bernard. I wish you'd come with us tonight, to see for yourself what he's like."

Mr. Potter had time only for a moment's sharp pang of disappointment before Wagstaff said, "Marry the guy if you like. But don't expect to number me among his admirers. These bright-eyed reformers! Though why is he so all-fired opposed to gambling when there are important things to worry about?"

Pat came to her fiancé's defense. "It takes too much money out of the working man's paycheck. But we've gone all over this before. It's no use talking." She sounded tired, as though the effort of defending Fullmer's viewpoint became exhausting. Her father was aware of her fatigue, too. "All right, dear. Don't worry about it." He smiled ruefully. "With the money I have tied up in race tracks, your husband will probably make me lose my shirt. But, after all, the money's for you, anyhow. If that's how you want it—"

She brushed her cheek against his. "Bless you," she said unsteadily.

The small French restaurant that Mr. Potter had chosen served perfect food and there was neither music nor floor show to distract his companion's attention. The Pat across a small table was unlike the Pat of parties. She was quieter, gentler. Watching her face now, it seemed to Mr. Potter that it was less vivid, that there was more than a touch of strain. Bayard the peerless was not making her happy. No wonder Wagstaff raged helplessly while he watched the man clipping his daughter's wings.

"It's odd, isn't it, Hiram," Pat said abruptly. "I was just thinking that we played together in the park when we were little, we've known each other all our lives, and yet how rarely we've ever just talked. You're very nice to talk to; you're interested."

The presence of the solitaire diamond on her left hand prevented him from saying how interested he was.

"You know what I think?" she asked.

He shook his head, smiling.

"I think that wolf pack at your house has been submerging you. Now that you're free, why don't you go out on your own, get away and find something to do that really fascinates you, something that is worth doing? In your position, I'd pack a bag tomorrow and go around the world."

Mr. Potter would have liked this better if he had not realized that Pat was comparing him with Fullmer who had found something worth doing. She made this plain.

"Bernard has set such a high goal for himself that, if he were anyone else, I'd worry about it. Such an enormous strain. But he is so disciplined and he sees so clearly what he wants."

"It's rather a strain for you, too, isn't it?" he said quietly.

She gave him an uncertain smile. "In a way," she admitted. "Caesar's wife and all that. He takes a lot of living up to. Of course, he's right. I am undisciplined. But I'll learn."

"He says you're undisciplined, does he?" Mr. Potter sounded grim.

"It's just that he has such flawless self-command himself," she said defensively. "You have no idea how hard he works. Everything he does is a step farther in his career. Everyone he knows—"

"It sounds just a shade cold-blooded."

"That," Pat explained, "is because you and I aren't ambitious. Lazy, really. Willing just to go along—"

Derogatory as the comment might be, Mr. Potter took comfort from it. You and I, she had said.

Pat looked at her watch. "We'll have to hurry! Bernard hates having people late. He's always on time himself."

"Does it matter so much?"

Pat met his eyes and to his surprise she blushed vividly, shamed by her own helpless infatuation. "Yes," she said flatly, "it matters. Bernard loves me but his career comes first. I guess it always will. He'd never forgive me if I hurt his career."

"Then we'd better hurry," Mr. Potter said grimly, "so you won't be late and make him angry."

III

The rally was being held in a small hall that

128

was dingy and uninviting. There was a flag-decked platform with a few uncomfortable chairs; a speaker's table with a glass of water, a pitcher and a microphone. A couple of hundred people had gathered and there was a whisper as Pat walked down the aisle. The papers had made much of her engagement to a man whose interests opposed her father's, indeed threatened them.

She chose a seat in the middle of the front row directly in front of the speaker's table. On each chair there was a folder with a picture of Bernard Fullmer, looking serious and dedicated, and a story of his life. He had come of poor but honest parents, worked his way through college where he had not only been a distinguished athlete but he had managed to keep his grades at scholarship level. He had been captain of the debating team as well as of the football team. He had been president of his senior class. He had been voted not only the best-looking man but the one most likely to succeed.

Politics had appealed to him, in spite of the many inviting offers he had received from business firms, as providing the most useful field for service. (Were there really people who said that sort of thing about themselves, Mr. Potter wondered.) Without money or influence, he was entering the political arena with clean hands, with the hope of contributing to good government in his city and destroying the pernicious influence of gambling rings.

Mr. Potter had barely time to be edified by reading the life story of Bernard Fullmer before a half-dozen men walked onto the platform, a couple of local party leaders, several minor politicians in need of publicity, and Bernard Fullmer, handsome, serious, dedicated, very sure of himself, with all the earmarks, Mr. Potter told himself in dejection, of a winning candidate. Pat leaned forward, caught his eye and smiled radiantly.

The first speech was a flag-waving affair, remarkable only for the number of clichés that could be packed into ten minutes. The second speaker introduced the men who were keeping in the public eye for strategic reasons, asked earnestly for a hand for each, which the docile audience gave them, and then introduced Bernard Fullmer.

He came forward, smiled at Pat, looked out over the audience, smiled again. The smile faded and he became serious as befitted the occasion.

It was, on the whole, a good speech. All that made Mr. Potter uncomfortable was that it seemed a trifle big for the occasion. It might have been given at Madison Square Garden or over a national hook-up. It was hard to remember that there were only a couple of hundred party henchmen in the audience and that the issue at stake was a comparatively minor city job, not one on which hinged international decisions.

Fullmer's delivery was excellent, his choice of words simple, although he did not make the mistake of talking down. He made no mistakes. His manner was easy but serious. He spoke for exactly the right length of time. He stopped to an enthusiastic outburst of applause.

Mr. Potter expected that Pat would dart forward to talk to her fiancé; instead, the evening provided him with an extra bonus.

"What do we do now, Hiram? Bernard has to see some of these men and he can't take me home."

"Do you want to dance?" Mr. Potter asked.

She refused regretfully. "I'd love to, but Bernard says it won't do. Now that he is becoming known and people have heard of our engagement, it would cause gossip if I went dancing with another man."

"Then let's go for a drive," Mr. Potter said. "In fact, we are going for a drive and I don't want to hear a word out of you."

He turned the nose of the car uptown, west

to the Henry Hudson parkway and along the river. On one side were the lights from the apartment buildings lining Riverside Drive, on the other the flashing signs of the Jersey shore. In the distance hung the lights of the lyric span of the George Washington bridge, muted by mist.

After a long silence Pat said, "It was a good speech, wasn't it?"

"A very good speech."

"Then why didn't you like it?"

"I find it difficult to believe all the right is on one side. Labels are simplifying but rather confusing, it seems to me."

"Bernard says that attack is the best defense." Pat leaned her head back against the seat. "You know, Hiram, it's very restful to drive with you. You aren't a demanding person."

Mr. Potter did not want to be restful. He gave the wheel a savage twist as they turned onto the Sawmill Parkway and pressed on the gas. The speedometer leaped from a decorous forty to fifty, to sixty, to seventy. With the car racing ahead, with Pat beside him, he was deeply content. She was there. They were together — well, in a way. When she was so quiet it was difficult to know where her thoughts were.

The peace was broken by an explosion and

Mr. Potter eased on his brake as the car ahead swerved out of control. The driver pulled to the side of the road and got out. Mr. Potter automatically drew up behind him.

"Need any help?"

The driver looked in the trunk, muttered to himself, came back to the sedan. "One of my kids took out the jack. Have you−?"

"Of course." Mr. Potter unlocked the trunk of the sedan, lifted the lid. He stood there for what seemed to him all eternity. Then, as lights loomed up from a car behind, he hastily took out the jack and dropped the lid.

He was more of a hindrance than a help in changing the tire. When the other man had thanked him and gone on he returned the jack. Thomas was still there, curled up in the trunk, his wide-open eyes fixed on Mr. Potter's face.

Chapter 9

The normal thing to do when you find a dead body in the trunk of your car is to inform the nearest policeman. Mr. Potter was perfectly aware of that fact. But he had heard of a woman's sensibilities all his life. His mother, his aunt and his cousin Deborah had made a career of their sensibilities. To tell Patricia Wagstaff bluntly that Thomas's corpse was curled up in the back of the car was unthinkable.

He made a U turn and started back to the city. Pat glanced at him once and then made no comment on their change of direction. Ever since the rally she had been depressed, disinclined to talk. Mr. Potter discovered a senseless kind of hope welling in his breast. Perhaps she was beginning to wonder how long she could endure listening to Bernard's speeches. If her vivid quality was already being dimmed, the flame quenched by her engagement, what would marriage do to her? He stole a quick look at the quiet face that was drawn, almost haggard, and could not feel sorry. He did not want to hurt her but he desperately wanted her free.

While he drove he grappled with the problem of Thomas's death, Thomas's most unwelcome presence in the car. His cousin had taken out the sedan — well, when? — any time after his own noisy return to the house two nights before. The car had been returned sometime that day. In the interim, someone had murdered Thomas. For he had not beaten himself to death with Mr. Potter's own wrench and then tucked himself into the trunk of the car.

Mr. Potter remembered Deborah saying that Thomas had taken a telephone call that night and then recalled answering the phone and hearing only the sound of breathing at the other end of the wire. He had, it occurred to him, probably been listening to the breathing of the person who had pushed poor Jennie out of an office window, who intended to silence Thomas forever.

But who had taken the chance of returning the car and why had it been done? And where had the car been in the meantime? Certainly it would have been less risky to leave it somewhere else. Gramercy Park is not a busy thoroughfare; it is, indeed, a little backwater of the city, passed by in the northward rush of progress. Anyone parking a car in front of the house took a terrible risk of being seen.

Mr. Potter realized that he was more perplexed by the return of the car with its grisly burden than he was by Thomas's violent end. There was nothing particularly startling in the idea that someone felt an irresistible urge to murder Thomas. The cache of twenty-five hundred dollars was a sound enough motive. Blackmail is an invitation to murder. The blackmailer fastens on his victim like a barnacle, inescapable and eternal.

Why, Mr. Potter wondered, had he never before given thought to Thomas's financial acumen? It should have occurred to him long since that even the most careful management could not have stretched the sixty dollars a week Amanda Potter had given her nephew to cover his night clubs, his cases of pinchbottle scotch.

Mr. Potter's face hardened as he remembered Thomas's repulsively boyish ways and thought of the fear on which he must have battened, the desperation he must have caused. And yet murder cannot be condoned.

Pat was silent until they reached the apartment building on Seventy-second Street. She seemed tired and out of spirits and her invitation to come in for a night cap was only half hearted. Mr. Potter refused, saw her to the door of the building, and then drove south. On Twenty-second Street he drew up before the precinct police station. The man at the desk looked up when he went in. Mr. Potter took comfort from the fact that O'Toole was not there.

"My name is Potter. Hiram Potter. I live—"

"Yeah, I know. We get about a call a day from your house."

Mr. Potter flushed.

"Well, what is it now?"

"The fact is — you'd better come out and take a look. There's a body in the trunk of my car."

"There's a — what?"

"A body. It's my cousin, Thomas Burkett. He has been murdered."

"The man who was reported missing?" The sergeant was already across the room, opening the door. Mr. Potter handed him the key and the sergeant unlocked the trunk. For a long moment he stared at the quiet body whose wide-open eyes stared back at him unblinking; then he closed the trunk and went back to telephone.

"Now then," he said to Mr. Potter, who told him about his aunt's alarm the day before, about the disappearance and return of the car with the key still in it, about his discovery of the body when he stopped to lend a jack to a driver on the highway.

While the sergeant took notes he studied Mr. Potter in swift, keen glances. "Quite a lot been happening at your house lately." He added with a shade of regret, "Pity O'Toole's on vacation. He shoulda been in on this."

Mr. Potter sat down. He discovered that he was shaking. A number of men arrived, piling out of cars: a doctor, photographers, a sketch artist, fingerprint men. Mr. Potter watched them, impressed by their swift but unhurried efficiency. All the machinery of modern criminal investigation had been set to work to determine the facts in the death of Thomas Burkett. It was impersonal machinery, far reaching. As a citizen, Mr. Potter was pleased; as Thomas's cousin, as — inevitably — a suspect, he was uneasy.

Two people had come to violent ends within forty-eight hours, and each of them involved the Gramercy Park house. The police could hardly fail to seek a connection between the two events. Mr. Potter was in a quandary. If he were to say, "I talked to Jennie Newcomb before her death; I am convinced that she was murdered," Mrs. Newcomb would come forward with her story that he had been the man who had driven the girl to suicide. If he were to point out that Thomas had an unexplained cache of twenty-five hundred dollars in small bills, that he was probably a blackmailer, the obvious victim was Mr. Potter himself.

He had no proof that Thomas had known Jennie's identity, nothing but a look of fleeting recognition and satisfaction seen by no one else. He had not proof that Jennie had been murdered, nothing but his own impression of her character and the testimony of Sam Trumble and Opal Reed, neither of whom would carry much weight in a court of law. A con man and a model. Against him was his public quarrel with Thomas and his rash statement to Tito that he had settled Thomas's hash. Against him were the scratches on his face. Against him was the bitter hostility of his aunt and of Deborah, and their unconcealed wish to remove him as an obstacle between them and the Potter money.

He was alarmed. When the activity on the sidewalk had ceased, when his car with its silent passenger had been driven away, a lieutenant of detectives took the sergeant's place at the desk and politely asked him to have his fingerprints taken.

Lieutenant Jones might have been the invisible man, average height and coloring, average features, average business suit and conservative necktie. He smiled in a friendly way. "Well, Mr. Potter," he said, "let's see what we can find out. When did your cousin disappear?" As he studied Mr. Potter's face he looked faintly puzzled.

"We don't know. When I went out yesterday afternoon I looked for the car. It was gone."

"Your cousin had the use of the car?"

"Both my cousins. As a matter of fact, I rarely drive it myself. When I returned late last evening, the sedan was outside the house. My aunt told me then that Thomas had not been home all day, had not telephoned about dinner. She was alarmed. I wasn't much concerned because she is easily alarmed."

The sergeant, who was taking notes, nodded rather grimly over this. "Called here regularly," he put in for the lieutenant's information. "Children making too much noise in the park, people loitering on the sidewalk and casing the joint."

"Were they?" the lieutenant asked, interested.

The sergeant snorted.

"Anyhow," Mr. Potter said, "the car had been returned so I assumed that my cousin had come home without my aunt hearing him and gone out again. But I suppose—"

The lieutenant nodded. "He'd been dead thirty-six to forty-eight hours. They'll be able to cut down the time later, of course." He read a slip on which the sergeant had scribbled, looked surprised. "You last saw your cousin — when?"

Mr. Potter sighed. "Night before last. He let me in when I — as a matter of fact, I was drunk."

"Drunk and disorderly," the sergeant said. "Disturbing the peace. O'Toole reported."

Lieutenant Jones looked still more surprised. "Were you on good terms with your cousin?"

"I told him what I thought of him," Mr. Potter said helplessly, "as O'Toole and a newspaper man will probably report to you, but I didn't kill him, lieutenant. I didn't so much as touch him."

"Where did you get those scratches?"

Mr. Potter put up one hand to his face. "Shaving, yesterday morning. I had a hangover and my hand wasn't too steady."

"Where were you when you discovered your cousin's body?"

"On the Sawmill River Parkway, about four miles beyond the second toll gate."

The lieutenant waited but Mr. Potter had nothing more to contribute.

"How did you happen to find it?"

Mr. Potter explained about the man with the

blowout and fortunately was able to remember the license number of the car.

"Just out for a drive?"

"Yes."

"Why did you wait to report the murder?" When Mr. Potter was silent he asked, "Were you alone?"

"There was a young lady with me, an old friend of the family. I didn't want to involve her in anything so ugly."

"You didn't tell her about your discovery?" The lieutenant was incredulous.

"Good God, no! Look here, lieutenant, she didn't know anything about it. Can't she be spared any publicity?" If Pat were to appear in the papers in any connection, however remote, with a murder, Fullmer would let her feel the full weight of his displeasure and she would blame him for it; she would never forgive him.

"We'll keep her out of it if we can. But this is murder, Mr. Potter. Her name, please?"

Feeling sick at his own impotence, Mr. Potter said, "Patricia Wagstaff." He gave the number of the apartment building on East Seventy-second Street.

The telephone rang and the lieutenant listened, making such unrevealing comments as, "I see...well, well...not at the present time..."

When he turned back to Mr. Potter he made no further reference to Pat. "How long have the Burketts lived at your house?"

"About ten years," Mr. Potter said drearily. "My mother took them in when Burkett died."

"According to your mother's will, I understand that her estate goes to you but that you are to provide her sister and your cousins with a home. That it?"

The call must have come from the house. That meant the news had been broken to his aunt and to Deborah; it meant they had been talking. Turning his drunken threats against Thomas into action? Suggesting he had hammered Thomas on the head and then stuffed him into the back of his own car?

Mr. Potter straightened up, a rabbit, the lieutenant thought, but a maddened rabbit. "A home, yes. But I informed my aunt yesterday that no particular home had been indicated. I asked her to move as soon as possible."

The lieutenant made no comment. He looked down at his nicely kept hands. "Did your cousin have any enemies?"

Mr. Potter took the plunge. "All right, here it is." He told about the money he had found in Thomas's desk. "I don't know how you'd account for it but it looks to me like blackmail. The only source of income Thomas had was an allowance of sixty dollars a week my mother gave him."

"Did you plan to continue that allowance?"

"I did not."

"Blackmail," the lieutenant said thoughtfully.

"I think," Mr. Potter told him, "Thomas recognized the girl who fell from the office building on Fourth Avenue. The body dropped into our garden, you know. I saw his face when he looked at her. I realize that isn't evidence. But he knew who she was. He was scared out of his wits at first and then he was – pleased. I think he knew who killed her."

"The Newcomb case," the sergeant said and the lieutenant nodded.

"The girl's stepmother came to New York to identify the body."

"That's the one."

"But the girl left a suicide note," the lieutenant said, still speaking to the sergeant, ignoring Mr. Potter.

"Not suicide," the latter snapped. He told about Jennie following him into the park, about their conversation, about his disastrous meeting with Opal and Sam Trumble. "All right, I know I'm in a bad spot. But if you had seen the girl, if you had heard her. She was scared of the dark. She was a stupid kid, easy to influence. And obstinate in the way stupid people often

144

are. All she could see was a bonus, some money of her own. Damn it, lieutenant, Jennie Newcomb didn't throw herself out of a high window. She was killed by someone she was trying to help. And if you don't lock me up I'm going to find out who did it if it's the last thing I do."

"It might well be, you know," the lieutenant said evenly. "Better leave it to the professionals." He looked at Mr. Potter again and there was a change in his expression. "Lock you up, Mr. Potter?" he said in bland surprise. "You are free to go. Stay around town, of course, where we can get in touch with you. Sorry we'll have to impound your car for a day or so. Good night."

The dismissal was so abrupt that Mr. Potter was taken aback. He stood up, relieved to find that he had stopped shaking.

"Good night, lieutenant. Good night, sergeant." He found himself outside the police station. The black sedan was gone. Only one person was on the street, a man who had cupped his hands to light a cigarette, concealing his face. He took the same direction Mr. Potter did.

At the corner of Twenty-first Street Mr. Potter stopped abruptly. The quiet of Gramercy Park was disturbed by the press cars parked on both sides of the narrow one-way street; cameras were in readiness; men lounged and laughed and looked at the house. From somewhere, nowhere, a curious crowd had collected to gape at the windows, although it was nearly two in the morning. A man had died by violence and people had collected to stare at the place where x marked the spot as though it were a television screen. All that was lacking, Mr. Potter thought with swift anger, was a singing commercial.

He went on to the alley, picked his way around ashcans in the dark, found the break in the hedge and crossed the tiny garden. He tapped softly at the basement door which opened cautiously on a chain.

"Who's there?"

"Let me in, Tito."

There was a muttered exclamation and the chain was released. Mr. Potter went inside.

"I thought you'd been arrested." Tito propelled Mr. Potter into his own room in the front part of the basement where drawn shades shut out the curious eyes of the waiting camera men, hoping to follow up their pictures of Mr. Potter in jail, Mr. Potter drunk, with Mr. Potter as kin to the dead; perhaps, who knew, Mr. Potter, murderer.

Antonia, in a tentlike blue flannel robe, gave a choked exclamation and flung her ample arms around Mr. Potter, kissed him with garlicy breath, and then stepped back in awful embarrassment.

"I didn't mean — oh, Mr. Potter — but that old fool Tito talked too much to the police and I thought you'd been locked up. I told Tito I'd leave him if you had."

Mr. Potter smiled at them both, his eyes twinkling. He let Antonia push him into a chair. She stood with her head on one side, the faint mustache showing on her upper lip, examining him as though searching for signs of the third degree.

"I'll get you something to drink," she said in a hushed tone. "We'd better keep our voices down or they will hear." She ducked her head toward the ceiling. "Such goings on. The police and then the doctor. He gave Mrs. Burkett a shot to stop her screaming and she's quiet now. But Miss Burkett is still up and prowling around. She's been ringing for me about every fifteen minutes, wanting one thing and another."

She handed him a glass of red wine and glared at Tito who sat with bowed head. "What did they do to you over there at the police station?"

"Just questioned me," Mr. Potter said mildly. "They have to do that, you know."

Tito looked up like a chastised dog, looked down, shuffled his feet.

"You old fool," Antonia said.

Tito's arms went out in a despairing gesture. "I wouldn't say anything to harm you, Mr. Potter. You know that. After the way you got your mother to hire us when she said she wouldn't have Italians, after the way you've tried to make things nice, after the way you covered up for me that time I had too much wine—"

Mr. Potter grinned. "Don't worry about it. You must tell the police anything they want to know. Don't try to lie to them."

Antonia sat down and leaned forward, hands on her spread knees, big breasts falling forward under the flannel robe which, to Mr. Potter's alarmed eyes, seemed too flimsy to contain them. "And did you really find Mr. Burkett dead in the trunk of your car?"

Mr. Potter nodded.

"And he'd been there all the time." Antonia brooded. "You want to look out for them," she said, jerking her head ceilingward. "They'd make you trouble if they could."

"Oh, look here, they can't possibly believe I killed Thomas."

"You can't tell what they believe. And it's not just because of Mr. Burkett either. It's the money. Money can do bad things to people. And you stand between them and the money."

"You must not say things like that," Mr.

Potter warned her.

"Just the same." Antonia said darkly. "I heard what she told the police about you driving them out and threatening her son and coming home drunk after being arrested with a naked model and criminals and all. It sounded bad to anyone who didn't know better."

Mr. Potter finished his wine. "You go to bed, both of you. And you'd better sleep late in the morning. We've all had a bad night. Anyhow, my aunt and cousin probably won't wake early after all this. They certainly won't want you again tonight."

The service bell rang shrilly.

Chapter 10

"I'll answer it," Mr. Potter said. "You two go to bed." He stood up, smiling faintly. "And thank you." He clapped Tito on the shoulder and went up the stairs to the drawing room.

No woman, he sometimes thought, could look as unalluring as Deborah. She ran to pastel shades that gave her a prematurely faded look. Tonight, in a pale blue negligee, her hair stringy under a washed-out ribbon, her face swollen with tears, she was disastrously un-attractive.

He was sorry for her in a dutiful sort of way but he could not bring himself to regret Thomas — although he regretted the manner of his death — and he had no great faith in the strength of Deborah's attachment to her brother. She had always resented the fact that he was so obviously his mother's darling. In some in-tangible way it had seemed almost as though she feared him. None the less, his death had been a great shock, an ugly shock. Even if one hated Thomas one would not want to see him as Mr. Potter had last seen him, the boyish look gone forever, an old-looking young man with the empty staring eyes of a statue, and the top of his head – Mr. Potter drew back from his thoughts.

"The Petrellas have gone to bed," he said gently. "Can I do anything for you?"

Deborah was standing listlessly in front of the grate, though the fire had gone out. Her cardtable lay on its side, the cards scattered over the rug, mute reminder of the moment when she had been informed of Thomas's murder.

"So the police let you go," she said. Her pale eyes became somewhat fixed. She was working herself up to hysterics. Oh, not tonight, Mr. Potter thought, fatigue dragging at him like a weight. Not tonight.

"You won't get away with it!" Her voice rose. "You killed Thomas. You killed him. Murderer! Murderer!" Her voice was almost a shriek.

Mr. Potter slapped her across the cheek. She caught her breath and staggered backward.

"Sorry, I didn't want to hurt you, just to stop the hysterics. Take a long breath. That's it." He eased her into a chair and went out to the kitchen where he heated some milk. He came back with the glass which he placed in her hand.

"Now then," he said. "I know what a shock this has been to you and your mother. I am sorry for your grief. But you must not say that I killed Thomas. It's nonsense and you know it. I can't pretend that I liked him; I never have pretended to like him. But, beyond wanting him out of the house, I wouldn't have done him any harm. You are perfectly aware of that, Deborah."

His eyes met hers steadily for a moment. "Drink your milk; it will help you to sleep."

Deborah sipped at it, set the glass on the table. "You quarreled with him."

"Oh, yes," he admitted wearily, "I quarreled with him."

"No one else hated him."

"Someone did," Mr. Potter told her with unexpected tartness. "Someone has been paying Thomas blackmail, and a blackmailer has never been a loveable character."

There was unbelieving contempt on Deborah's face. "Of all the filthy things to say—"

"Then how," Mr. Potter asked her, "did Thomas get the twenty-five hundred dollars I found in his desk drawer this afternoon?"

"Thomas never had that much money in his

life." Slowly his words penetrated. "What did you say? I don't believe it."

"It's there," Mr. Potter said in his quiet voice, "and he didn't save it out of his allowance. He didn't save anything. I should have realized long ago that Thomas had some source of income he didn't care to mention."

"If he had that much money in his room you put it there!" Hatred twisted her mouth but her voice was low in order not to awaken her mother. "You've been trying to plant evidence to blacken Thomas, to make people think he had an enemy."

Mr. Potter sighed. "You'll really have to do better than that. You know how my money reaches me every month. There isn't a penny that can't be accounted for. Wagstaff sees to that."

Deborah's brows drew together. He watched her grapple with the information he had given her, wondering how much she had known or guessed of her brother's activities.

Some of the hysterical rage she had tried to whip up died away. She was, he saw, attempting honestly to evaluate the situation.

"I don't understand this at all," she admitted at length. "What do you think, Hiram?" She looked at him for the first time as though she were consulting a friend, not confronting an enemy. "What do the police think?"

"They didn't say . . . That's right, finish your milk. But two murders tied up with this house within three days are too much for anyone to swallow, unless there is some vital connection between them."

He would have taken his oath that this idea came as a genuine surprise to her. "The girl who fell in the garden? But the papers said it was suicide! And if — Thomas couldn't have pushed her out of the office window. He was right here in the house."

"I think he suspected who had pushed her. He recognized that girl, Deborah. I saw his face when he looked at her."

"You could never prove a beastly thing like that."

"If there is any connection between the two deaths, the police will find it. I watched them at work tonight. They are highly competent men. Don't let yourself be fooled by people who write them off as dubs. Personally, I think the connection lies somewhere in the building where the girl fell. I think she was killed by someone who was familiar with the building, someone whom Thomas may have seen at some time at the Morland penthouse."

Deborah was thoughtful, searching her own memories.

"Morland himself?" she asked, confused. "If you're right, there was something – I told you he was amused after he went to Morland's party. And then–" her voice trailed off, grew stronger again – "then he fitted up that little theater in the basement." For a moment her tongue licked out between her pale lips. "If mother only knew!"

"Not Morland. He is in Paris. It must be someone who was here in the house the day of Mother's funeral, because that day our park key disappeared from the hook in the front hall. In other words, the murderer seems to narrow down to one of two people: Wilbur Wagstaff or Bernard Fullmer, and I think Thomas knew which one, demanded money to keep still, got paid and then was killed so he would make no more demands."

The glass slopped over as Deborah set it down. "I didn't know anyone could be so vile!" Her moment of tentative trust was gone. "Because you are jealous of Bernard Fullmer. Because you want to undermine a man whose shoes you aren't fit to tie. What good do you think it would do you? Even with your money do you think Pat would ever look at you? Do you know what you are? A laughing stock, that's what! A laughing stock!"

She stopped for breath, gathering ammunition, seeking for the thing that would hurt him most. "You can't equal Bernard in any way so you want to drag him into the dust. Isn't it bad enough that he should be involved with Pat? Now you want to destroy him. Well, you can't do it. That's all. I'll never let you do it."

He was taken aback by her frenzy. Fretful and querulous he had known her to be, given to self-pity and self-dramatization, but he had never guessed at this wildness of untamed emotion.

"What's Fullmer to you?" he asked.

"I love him," Deborah said with a gesture that would have been worthy of Mrs. Siddons, but which he did not find amusing. No one could have mistaken its sincerity. "I've loved him from the first time I ever saw him. I'd do anything for him, anything! When I think of him marrying that girl who doesn't understand or appreciate him, it's enough to drive me mad. She doesn't care about his career, only his handsome looks. And she'll destroy him. The only way she can help him is with her money; if I had that much I could do more for him. I'd entertain the right people for him instead of laughing at them the way she does, or looking down my nose. I'd devote my life to his interests!"

Oddly enough, Mr. Potter believed there was

an element of truth in this. In some ways, Deborah would make the better wife for Fullmer; not so glamorous as to arouse suspicion; a patient, tireless worker, an uncritical worshiper. Fullmer's constant nobility would not be the strain it was to Pat; Deborah would thrive on a diet of nobility.

"Anyhow," she pounced on the obvious point, "even if Thomas were a blackmailer, he could not blackmail Bernard. Not just because he had led a blameless life but for the simple reason that the poor boy has no money except for a small salary in a law office. He doesn't have sums like twenty-five hundred dollars lying around."

Mr. Potter was interested to note that, when it came to the pinch, Deborah was more inclined to defend Fullmer than her brother. Evidently, she was not finding it impossible to believe that Thomas had been blackmailing someone.

"If it's anyone," she went on, "if Thomas did a thing like that, it's Wilbur Wagstaff. He has money, heaven knows. Otherwise, Bernard couldn't have afforded to marry Pat. And there would be plenty of reasons for blackmailing Wagstaff or his angel daughter, for that matter! Wagstaff's an old goat with his women! And he can't afford any scandal about them because

Bernard would never marry Pat if there were any scandal. It would sacrifice his career." She licked her lips nervously.

"Wagstaff—" she was speaking more slowly now. "He was downright worried about Pat or he'd never have given his consent to her engagement to Bernard. He thinks she'll be safe with a man like that, even if Bernard's election should mean a financial loss. He's got a lot of money tied up in race tracks and Bernard hates betting. If he's elected, he'll try to clean up the whole thing. You can see yourself how important Wagstaff thinks it is for Pat to marry or he wouldn't put up with Bernard. He'd be mighty tough on anyone who tried to break up Pat's marriage. He'd hate to have Bernard find out about Pat's previous marriage. Thomas dropped a hint to him—" she caught herself — "oh, jokingly, of course—" she stopped.

She looked at Mr. Potter and smiled. This time, her look said, it's really going to hurt. "You know Pat fell wildly in love with a gangster. He didn't want to get mixed up with any girl but she chased him. She was the one who wanted to get married. They eloped and Wagstaff found out and had the marriage annulled. Pat never forgave Thomas for telling her father. She has always hated him. She hates us all and she'd like to get even. I suppose she is the one who put you up to trying to drive us out of the house."

There was no expression on Mr. Potter's face and Deborah felt uneasily that the bullet she had fired was proving to be a dud.

At length he asked, "How did Thomas hear about this — marriage of Pat's?"

Deborah's expression was almost a smirk. "I was down at City Hall. My classmate, June Baker, was getting her marriage license and they came out of the little chapel. I told Thomas."

She finished her drink, set the glass down, sloppily wiped the spilled milk off the table with the sleeve of her negligee, leaving a white smear.

Mr. Potter got to his feet with his easy, unobtrusive courtesy. For a long moment she stood looking at him, a look of such hatred and malice that Mr. Potter felt cold. He met her eyes steadily. She was the first to turn away.

"I'll tell you this, Hiram," she said. "Thomas wouldn't have been driven to doing — anything bad, if he had had some money of his own. But he didn't get a cent of the Potter money. None of us got a cent. He was forced into it — you forced him into it."

II

Mr. Potter was too tired to go to bed, too tired to get out of the chair in which he had sat since Deborah had gone upstairs. Too tired to think. The telephone bell shocked him to his feet. He glanced at the long clock in the hall. Nearly three-thirty. He reached the telephone before it would ring a second time.

"Oh, thank goodness, it's you," said Opal Reed, a touch of hysteria in her voice.

Mr. Potter braced himself. "What's wrong?"

"It's the police. They've just left but there is a plainclothes man outside watching the house. I can see him from the window. They came here to ask me about your cousin."

"About Thomas?" Even in his astonishment, Mr. Potter remembered to keep his voice low, though there was not much likelihood that the conversation could be overheard behind the closed door of Deborah's room on the third floor.

"It is true he was found murdered in the trunk of your car?"

"Yes, but what on earth are you supposed to know about it?"

"It's because of all that publicity about the Gink Club raid and the police know we were all together and that Jennie was my roommate.

160

They are after Sam, just because he has a record. They think you hired Sam to – to do it." She was crying now, but trying to steady her voice.

"But that's preposterous. Why would I want Thomas killed? And why, even if I did, would I want to tuck his body away in the back of my own car where anyone could have found it?"

"Of course it's silly. Only if they search this place, it's going to be just too bad because Sam was hiding in the closet all the time they talked to me. And I can't go on hiding him here."

"Certainly not." Mr. Potter was shocked at the idea. "But why didn't he come and talk to the police? Why go into hiding?"

"Because they'd arrest him. There's no telling what they would do to him."

Opal's idea was that she would leave her apartment, acting very suspiciously, and draw the detective away. Then Sam would be free to go to Mr. Potter's without any risk of being followed.

"You want me to hide him here?" Mr. Potter was startled.

"Well – not if you're afraid."

"Tell him to come along." Mr. Potter gave her instructions in a low tone and put down the telephone. He was not at all tired. He went back to the drawing room, switched off the

161

lights and stood at the window, watching a camera man who still continued his vigil, wondering what he expected would happen. Of course, with one body behind the house and one in front of it within so short a space of time, the fellow might be expecting that violence had become the pattern. And he might be right, Mr. Potter admitted to himself. He too had an uneasy feeling that it was not over.

The crowd of curious had drifted away and there were no lights except for those outside the Gramercy Park Hotel and the red warning lamps set up to discourage inebriated motorists from crashing through the iron gates into the park.

For a long time Mr. Potter looked at the park, remembering Jennie's fear of the dark. "My stepmother—" There was a lot he wanted to know from Sam Trumble about Mrs. Newcomb. No one was paying sufficient attention to the woman: She had knowledge that must be forced out of her. Dangerous knowledge, as Thomas's had been dangerous to him. Too much time had been wasted.

The night – the morning, he corrected himself, for it was after four o'clock now – was incredibly still, though there was the distant muffled rumble of the city that is never at rest. Mr. Potter looked at his watch and hastily abandoned his vigil at the window. He removed his shoes and carefully negotiated the uncarpeted basement stairs. For a moment he paused outside the Petrellas' room where the sound of their heavy breathing reassured him. They were unlikely to awaken. He went on down to the end of the hall, slipped off the chain and opened the door.

The garden was dark. In the office building across the alley lights burned in an office where, presumably, cleaning women were still at work. On Fourth Avenue, the traffic signal changed from red to green, throwing a reflection on the scrap of sidewalk visible to Mr. Potter.

Something rustled and he stood motionless. He felt the wind crisp and cool on his face. Probably it had stirred dead autumn leaves under the trees. He was getting over-imaginative, he told himself impatiently. And yet he felt acutely that he was not alone. As though someone were sharing his vigil in the darkness.

And then in the green space a man moved, darted into the alley. In a few moments a shadow stirred in the garden and Sam Trumble slipped through the open door and at Mr. Potter's whispered suggestion, took off his shoes. They tiptoed in silence up to the main floor where Mr. Potter mixed each of them a drink and they conferred in whispers.

"I wasn't followed," Sam said. "I saw the detective go after Opal. She'll shake him at Times Square. Nice of you to take me in. How are you going to prevent your family from knowing I am here?"

"I'll put you in my mother's room and give you a key. Keep the door locked. There's a bathroom that opens into my room. Better not turn on any water unless I am in my room."

There was amusement in the curve of Sam's amiable mouth. "Quite a conspirator, aren't you?"

Mr. Potter yawned. He showed his guest to his mother's room, handed him the key and waited until it turned softly in the lock. Then he stumbled into his own room. He was asleep almost as soon as he got into bed.

Chapter 11

Sam Trumble closed the door, turned the key in the lock as softly as possible and switched on the lights. The late Mrs. Potter's bedroom was not only high ceilinged but surprisingly large, larger even than the drawing room on the floor below, extending back for almost two-thirds the length of the house, leaving space only for Mr. Potter's small room at the back, and a bath between.

There was a big four-poster bed with a satin canopy, a large fireplace, massive chairs upholstered in petit point, heavy velvet draperies drawn over the high windows and sweeping the polished floor. Everything was outsize, everything was gloomy and, in spite of the large furniture, the room had an empty, almost an unfurnished appearance. But Sam was impressed. His world, as long as he could remember, had been one of impermanence and improvisation, of furnished rooms, of drifting from place to place. Amanda Potter's bedroom not only had an air of permanence, it seemed to have been there for generations. There was, Sam thought, something comforting about being rooted. Nor did the ugliness of the room disturb him. Bigness in itself had a kind of virtue in his eyes. Hiram Potter, he realized, was a far more wealthy man than he appeared to be.

Sam smiled as he thought of Mr. Potter. You never could tell. His face was mild, his voice quiet, his manners deprecating. But the quiet voice spoke its owner's mind and the retiring fellow seemed to be on hand when you needed him. There was, Sam decided, quite a bit more to that young man than appeared on the surface. He had taken Sam's police record in his stride, saying nothing but that it seemed to him rather lonely. Lonely. Sam considered the word. That was what Opal kept hammering at; nice girl, Opal. The kind you could depend on. If he were a marrying man with a settled income — but he wasn't a marrying man and nothing about him was settled, including the immediate future.

He sobered. In the course of a highly unorthodox career he had never before so much as brushed the skirts of murder. But Jennie had been murdered, Jennie who had been Opal's roommate, Jennie whose only New York acquaintance he had been. And on top of that, this fellow Burkett. Someone was playing for keeps.

Sam undressed slowly, took his time over a hot bath, pulled pajamas and a clean shirt out of his briefcase and, after a last peek out of the window at the patient photographer who had crawled back into his car to doze, he went to bed.

As a rule, a sound digestion and a clear conscience were Sam's best safeguards against insomnia, but murder was different. There was no doubt, from the questions he had heard the police ask Opal that night, that a movement was on foot to throw the blame for Thomas Burkett's murder on Mr. Potter, and that Sam and Opal would be dragged into the case.

Sam thought better when he was smoking and he started to swing his legs out of bed to go in search of a cigarette when something brushed against the door. Potter, he thought. He can't sleep and he wants to talk. Sam got out of bed, groped his way to the door, eased it open. There was no one in the hall. The only sound was a faint creak. Someone on the stairs? Wood reflecting changing temperatures at night?

On the third floor a door closed softly. Sam went up the stairs, keeping to the outside of

167

the treads, his bare feet making no sound. At the top his foot came down heavily because he expected another step and he stopped short, listening. There were three doors on the third floor. It was the middle one which had closed.

Sam held his breath. What had Potter told him about the layout of the house? If he were walking in on one of the Burketts he might as well throw in his hand. No, this must be the late Thomas's room.

He opened the door inch by inch. The room was in darkness except for a flashlight which was turned on a desk drawer. The drawer closed, another was opened. Papers were turned over one at a time, each one carefully scanned.

Sam moved forward a cautious step, trying to see who held the flashlight. There was a faint creak as his weight shifted. The flashlight left the desk, played over the floor. Sam stood motionless, expecting that it would find his face. Then it returned to the desk and a stack of stationery. A hand moved, the stationery was lifted and Sam, peering forward, saw a pile of currency. He heard a gasp and then a hand closed over the roll of bills.

The sight of the money disappearing was too much for him. He took a step forward, lunged for the flashlight, fumbled it and it dropped, rolled toward his bare feet. The intruder brushed against him, running. Lurching forward, he cracked his head against the corner of the door. For a moment he saw stars and sagged forward. By the time his head had cleared he heard feet racing down the lower flight of stairs.

If he were to run in pursuit he might arouse the house; in any case, he had the money safe. Whoever it was would not dare go out the front door because of the press car. He looked out the back window, leaning far out. The sky was growing light but the garden was still in darkness. He saw a strip of sidewalk beyond the alley turn red and green as traffic signals changed. He watched for a long time. No one left the house.

Sam made his way down the stairs to Mrs. Potter's bedroom and sat on the side of the bed, smoking. The early morning was chilly and he drew up the covers . . .

Mr. Potter was shaking his shoulder. He sat up sleepily. He smelled coffee and bacon. Mr. Potter was setting a tray on the table beside the bed.

"I had Tito bring up my breakfast," he said. "Here you are. I'll get something for myself outside. Keep your door locked and the bathroom door too. I forgot about the bathroom door last night. Antonia might come in here when she does my room."

"You had an intruder," Sam told him. He reached out and gave Mr. Potter a fistful of bills from the table. "Tried to steal this." He described his pursuit in the night while he ate his breakfast.

"A burglar? But how did he get in?"

"Well, if anyone got in, it was probably through the door you let me in by. Did you remember to put on the chain?"

"I have no idea. But why Thomas's room? How would anyone know the money was there?"

"Whoever paid the money to Thomas in the first place would know. How many people have you told about finding it?"

"Wagstaff, his daughter, my cousin Deborah, the police."

Sam saved his big punch line for the knockout. "Well," he drawled, "I don't think she left the house."

"She!"

"Smelled the perfume," Sam said. "It was a woman, all right. She couldn't have gone out the front door because the press car was still there. And she didn't go out the back way. I watched for nearly thirty minutes."

"Deborah, then. But, why, in God's name?"

"Or her mother. Or your cook."

"Not Aunt Prudence because she was under an opiate. And certainly not Antonia because she is honest."

Sam laughed quietly. "Deborah, then," he said. "Those cousins of yours get their money the hard way."

"I don't believe it's the money for its own sake," Mr. Potter said. "It's the money as evidence that Thomas was a blackmailer. It's my proof that someone, aside from me, had reason for disliking him."

"But what could she gain by it?" Sam asked.

"If I go to the electric chair for Thomas's murder," Mr. Potter said grimly, "she gains the whole works." He was thinking hard. "Sam, you'd better put that money back where you found it, but be careful, for heaven's sake! If you are caught it will simply indicate that I am planting evidence." He picked up the tray. "I'll bring back some newspapers."

"Where are you going?"

"To get some breakfast. You've eaten mine. And then I'm going to buy a new car. I don't know when the police will release the sedan and anyhow I shouldn't care to drive it again. Every time I opened the trunk I'd see Thomas staring out at me."

Mr. Potter left the tray in his own bedroom and went downstairs. The photographer had

171

given up his vigil. In the basement, he passed the doors of the furnace room, storage rooms, Thomas's room for showing movies — the room, he recalled, that his cousin had equipped after his visit to Morland's penthouse in the fall — and went toward the door that opened on the garden. The chain was off. He must have forgotten it when he admitted Sam.

Standing there he remembered waiting for Sam the night before the curious impression he had had that someone was in the garden with him. Funny how the darkness could distort a man's judgment. He walked toward the tree where he had heard the rustling sound. There were plenty of autumn leaves, all right. There were also nearly a dozen cigarette butts.

Inside, the telephone rang insistently. Mr. Potter hesitated and then bent to pick up the cigarettes. While he crossed the strip of garden to the hedge the phone continued to ring.

II

The black sedan had been designed on handsome and conservative lines. The car which Mr. Potter purchased that morning was a long, raking convertible painted a screaming yellow with a black top. It was a car that insisted on being seen. Seated at its wheel Mr. Potter made the salesman think irresistibly of Snow White riding a prancing charger, a fancy that delighted him almost as much as the check for payment in full, which, according to a discreet telephone conversation with Mr. Potter's bank, was as sound as Fort Knox.

Unhappily, it was not a car in which anyone could creep unobserved onto Gramercy Park. It proclaimed itself proudly. Mr. Potter hunched over the wheel for a moment as he turned on Twenty-first Street. Then he straightened his shoulders, completed the turn, and slid smoothly into the curb.

Four people were standing in the open doorway of his house; Deborah, Pat Wagstaff, her father, and Bernard Fullmer. As they saw Mr. Potter's spectacular arrival the last three came down the steps toward him and Deborah went inside and slammed the door. Pat shrieked with delight over the yellow convertible.

Bernard Fullmer was finding it difficult to maintain his pleasant smile. He shook hands with Mr. Potter and thanked him for keeping Pat's name out of the papers, but he could not achieve any degree of cordiality. He looked as though he had not slept, a generally blurred expression destroyed his good looks. He and Wagstaff were maintaining their relations on even a thinner thread of good will than usual. Pat clung to his arm, watching his face anxiously.

Adam Faber drifted absentmindedly around the side of the park from the direction of the Players. His white hair was ruffled by the wind. His eyes were vague, absorbed in dreams. He aroused himself with a dramatic start that was pure ham, and bowed gallantly to Pat, turning so that his best profile was toward the others.

"Miss Wagstaff!" He beamed at her. "I see those lovely eyes of yours on that convertible. I suspect it won't be long until you persuade Mr. Potter to let you try it out."

Pat nodded vaguely and tucked her free hand under Mr. Potter's arm.

"Let's go inside," Fullmer said abruptly. "We're too conspicuous out here after all the publicity the house has had."

Adam Faber gave him a keen glance and his eyes twinkled.

Pat flushed, gave Mr. Potter a placating smile, and hastened up the steps with her fiancé.

Her father let out his breath in a long sigh. "What in the name of all that's unlikely does she see in him, Hiram? Half the time I think she is actually afraid of him." He stopped Mr. Potter as he was about to follow them up the steps. "I've been calling you all morning. Have you talked to your aunt since Thomas's body was found?"

Mr. Potter shook his head. "By the time I was through with the police last night – or they were through with me – Aunt Prudence was asleep. I went out early this morning. Had a couple of errands to do."

Wagstaff's eyes rested on the yellow convertible, turned to Mr. Potter with the expression of perplexity that was becoming habitual. "I want to talk to you before you see her, put you on your guard."

"Shall we go for a ride?"

"Not in that circus wagon of yours." Wagstaff was firm.

"I'll get the park key," Mr. Potter said absently. It was not until he actually found it hanging on its usual hook inside the door that he remembered it should not be there. He turned it over and over in his hand as though expecting to find some evidence of where it had been. Money in Thomas's desk where it should not have been, a park key hanging where it should not have been. Those were the only bits of evidence he had to connect the house on the park with two violent deaths. An attempt had failed to remove the money; an attempt had succeeded to return the key. But when had it been returned? He had not looked at the hook that morning. It might have been there. It might not.

The two men crossed the street, went inside the park and closed the gate. At this hour, there was no one inside but a hypochondriac from a building across the park who was grimly taking his morning constitutional as though it were an indigestible pill, plodding with dreary virtue along the paths.

"It was considerate of you," Wagstaff said abruptly, "not to let Pat know you had found Thomas's body in the car. I appreciate that."

"Natural thing to do," Mr. Potter assured him.

"Of course, it was a hell of a shock when the police came to the house to question her. She couldn't believe it at first. But I must say they are being very decent. They'll keep her name out of it if they possibly can. That's why Bernard came along. He wants to be sure her name isn't mentioned."

"He could hardly blame Pat if it was."

"He could make it damned unpleasant for her. Well, thank God, the morning papers say only that you found the body. But, of course, you've seen them."

"Just the headlines. I bought them all, they're in the car, but I haven't looked beyond the headlines yet. After Jennie's death and that Gink Club affair, it's becoming a carnival for the press."

Wheezing along at his side, Wagstaff asked, "Why didn't you call me as soon as you dropped Pat? I should have been on hand to advise you when you saw the police."

"At that point," Mr. Potter commented, "to arrive at the precinct station complete with a body and a lawyer would have been a bit thick."

"What did they ask you? What did you tell them?"

Mr. Potter reported it as accurately as he could. "Sorry I had to bring in Pat's name," he concluded.

"You did your best. She's all I have, Hiram. Maybe I've indulged her too much. It's hard to tell. But I can't bear to have her hurt. That stuffed shirt she is going to marry would have raised hell if he'd been involved in this mess."

Wagstaff shook his head. "I'd never have believed the day would come when Pat would fall in love with a hunk of civic virtue. Sure, he's a handsome fellow but he curbs my girl. She's afraid to do anything without thinking twice to see what its political implications would be; and worried half the time that Bernard won't approve of her. It's beginning to drag her down. Well—" he sighed and brushed aside his personal problem — "that's not why I wanted to see you."

It was too chilly to sit down and the two men walked briskly. "Look here," the lawyer said at length, "your aunt is going to make trouble for you, Hiram."

She had telephoned, he said, the night before, as soon as she had heard of Thomas's murder. She had been a mad woman, beside herself with shock and tempestuous grief and frenzied rage against her nephew.

"The long and short of it is that she's going to try to pin Thomas's murder on you. If she can't prove premeditation, she'll try for insanity; if she can't prove that, she'll settle for having you declared mentally incompetent. But she's going to make you suffer for Thomas's death."

Unobtrusively, Mr. Potter pulled out a handkerchief and patted his forehead, ran a hand over the silken smooth blond hair. If Wagstaff observed that his color had faded he made no comment.

"That's why I had to see you," the lawyer went on. "Prudence Burkett is a five-letter word so far as I am concerned, she always has been; but in a jury box she would be a bereaved mother. She's eminently respectable. She'd make an impression."

Mr. Potter had not spoken; for a moment the lawyer thought he was so lost in thought that he had not been attending to what he said.

"The damnable thing," Wagstaff broke out, "is that you have been behaving oddly since your mother's death."

There was a curious expression on Mr. Potter's face. "You are genuinely worried about this, aren't you, sir?"

"Naturally I'm worried," Wagstaff snapped. "You're my client and, damn it, I'm not a criminal lawyer. Mrs. Burkett telephoned again this morning. Deborah had told her about this business of Thomas blackmailing people — why the hell did you have to be so open and above board with her? Prudence would destroy you before she'd let you bring that out as a reason for her son's murder."

Wagstaff trotted beside Mr. Potter, small and square and more than a trifle breathless. The pouches in which his eyes were sunk looked as dark as though they had been bruised. The veins stood out on his face. Old and sick at heart and incompetent, Mr. Potter thought.

"This is the real problem," Wagstaff said at last. "Prudence has an alienist waiting for you at the house. He is supposed to look you over. I wish to God you could get away and stay away until after the inquest. Give me time to shake some sense into her."

Mr. Potter stopped to light a cigarette. He

inhaled deeply. Wagstaff gave him a troubled look. From this angle his face had more character than he had realized. He did not have a prognathous jaw, far from it, but it was not as yielding as one would expect, either. There were lines of decision on his face which the lawyer had never observed before.

"It's one hell of a mess," Wagstaff grunted, "but we'll straighten it out. Eventually. But meantime I want to keep you out of jail."

They had reached the east gate. Peering through it was the rather dirty face of a small boy. Mr. Potter looked around guiltily and then unlocked the gate. The boy slipped inside.

"Hiya, Hiram," he said. "Gee, what happened to you? The gang hasn't been able to get in since Monday."

"Mislaid the key," Mr. Potter explained. "No rough stuff now, Red."

"Well, we try to keep quiet, but that old lady at your house yaps if we make a sound. Like last Saturday. We were just trying out those stilts you gave us and Tom fell off and we were laffin' and she calls the cops."

"So you spoiled our hedge to get even."

The boy flushed as he met Mr. Potter's eyes. There was no friendly twinkle in them. "We didn't think of it as your hedge. Just hers. I'm sorry."

Mr. Potter smiled. "All right, but don't destroy any more property. You're on your honor when you're in here. When you misbehave you let me down pretty badly. Okay?"

"Okay."

Mr. Potter looked through the iron gate straight into the intent face of O'Toole, who sat in a shabby blue Plymouth of ancient vintage. That, he thought drearily, is all that was needed. I've been caught admitting Third Avenue kids to the park. Oh, hell!

He turned back to Wagstaff. "The park key was returned either last night or this morning. When I drove up just now, had Fullmer gone inside or was he still outside the house?"

Wagstaff answered quickly, "None of us had gone in. Deborah opened the door and then we saw you and came down."

"I see." Mr. Potter took a long breath. "I think," he said levelly, "I'll take your advice. I'd better not go back to the house. Will you do something for me? My friend, Sam Trumble, is hiding in Mother's room." He ignored the lawyer's startled exclamation. He explained what he wanted done and stood back to let the lawyer precede him through the west gate.

He watched the stout figure trot up the steps to the front door and then he got behind the wheel of the yellow convertible and drove slowly uptown. Near the ramp on Ninety-sixth Street leading up to the West Side Highway he parked the car and waited. Somehow he believed that Wagstaff would not fail him on this.

For over half an hour he sat motionless, his hands resting quietly on the wheel. Now and then people paused for a second look at the spectacular car and observed the intent face of the man in the driver's seat. Once his lips moved. "Deborah," he said.

A man who might be a college instructor came down the street, a briefcase in his hand. A girl in a red corduroy coat with an immense black patent leather handbag tucked under her arm and a suitcase in her hand, crossed the street. The two converged on the convertible and climbed in beside Mr. Potter.

He turned the key in the switch, turned the car onto the ramp. "Well," he said unsteadily, "we're off!" He managed a chuckle. "Alone at last."

Behind the yellow convertible came a shabby blue Plymouth.

Chapter 12

Past the second toll gate on the Sawmill River Parkway Mr. Potter came to the place where he had stopped to help the man with the blowout, where he had discovered Thomas's dead body curled up in the trunk of his car. He was so deep in thought that neither Opal nor Sam ventured to interrupt his meditations. Now and then they stole swift, speculative glances at him. Somehow, when they viewed him in this way, when they saw the line of his profile, of his jaw, rather than the mildness of his eyes and his innocuous expression, he seemed different. He was, they began to suspect, someone to reckon with.

Mr. Potter himself, beyond learning that Wagstaff had delivered his messages to them promptly and accurately, appeared almost to have forgotten their presence. Within the space of three days a great many things had happened, which he had not had time to digest.

The death of his mother had been followed by the reading of her will, which had saddled him with the Burketts for the rest of his life. The murder of Jennie on the night of his mother's funeral had involved the house on Gramercy Park; not merely because she had fallen into the garden behind the house but because, presumably, she had been led to her death by someone who had come out of the house and taken the key to the park. Someone, he recalled in perplexity, who had returned it within the past few hours.

"I should think," he said aloud abruptly, because the thought tormented him so much that he had to express it, "that it would be possible for a doctor to determine whether Jennie was dead before she fell or whether the fall killed her. If she was conscious, if she knew what was happening to her—" He remembered the faint cry that had made him look up and he broke off, his hands tightening on the wheel.

"Whatever they know," Sam said, "it's a cinch they won't take us into their confidence."

Mr. Potter withdrew into his thoughts. Thomas had recognized Jennie, had guessed how she had met her death and why she had had to die. He had blackmailed her murderer who had given him twenty-five hundred dollars and then silenced him. And how the police were attempting to find Mr. Potter guilty of plotting Thomas's murder, of using Sam as his tool in carrying out the actual killing. And if the police failed, Mr. Potter thought drearily, his aunt would try to have him declared mentally incompetent and locked up so that she could take over control of the Potter money.

Deborah would love that. She believed that the only thing that prevented her from taking Bernard Fullmer away from Pat was her lack of money to help build his career. For all he knew to the contrary, it might even be true. One of the most humiliating aspects of Pat's engagement was the obvious fact that she was more deeply in love than Fullmer. As bad as Deborah. She could see no fault in him. She was trying to make herself over to please him. Afraid of him, Wagstaff had hinted.

There were a number of urgent questions and Mr. Potter did not know the answer to any of them:

1. Who had been Jennie Newcomb's employer?

2. Whom had she met in the park?

3. When had the park key been replaced on its hook inside the door?

4. Who had driven the sedan back to the house with Thomas's dead body inside and why

had the car been returned?

5. Who had ransacked Thomas's room in the night and tried to take the money?

6. Who had bribed Mrs. Newcomb to identify ſennie's body and claim that she had committed suicide?

He asked his six questions aloud.

"I keep wondering about Jennie's boss," Opal said. "She got her job in an odd sort of way and didn't expect it to work out so well. That's all she ever said. If we're not wrong about everything, she must have been working either for Wagstaff or for Fullmer."

"That's the hitch," Mr. Potter told her. "Wagstaff has a very impressive office. There must be fifteen or twenty employees. Jennie couldn't have worked there without someone knowing about her."

"Then it must be Fullmer. Do you know where his office is?"

"Madison Avenue about Forty-fifth Street. I went there once with Pat — with Miss Wagstaff. A little room on a court. He shared a stenographer and office space with another young fellow. The stenographer was the kind you would expect a cautious fellow like Fullmer to pick out, a pleasant, middle-aged woman who was efficient and had good manners."

So they were back where they had started.

"And anyhow," Mr. Potter added sadly, "you can't get blood out of a turnip and Fullmer hasn't the kind of money someone handed out to Thomas."

Another possibility was beginning to torment him. If Fullmer himself had not been blackmailed, had it been Wagstaff? Had he been paying Thomas to keep still about some scandal in his life that would frighten Fullmer away from Pat? There was increasing evidence to support such a theory. Wagstaff adored his daughter. He would sacrifice anything – anyone – for her happiness. It was not too difficult to picture him killing Thomas.

For a moment Mr. Potter had a startlingly clear vision of Thomas with his little-boy smile threatening to make public some peccadillo of Wagstaff's and the lethal rage that would follow. It was not so easy, however, to picture the old man pushing Jennie out of a window. In fact, and considerably to his relief, Mr. Potter could not imagine it.

"No one," Opal said crisply, "could possibly be as noble as Fullmer. Everyone slips sometimes, even if it is just a small, harmless slip. If he is all they say, he is simply not human."

"No one ever suggested that he was," said Mr. Potter. At Hawthorne Circle he turned onto the Taconic Parkway.

"Where are we going?" Opal asked.

"A shack I own in the Connecticut hills. I used it for a weekend place for awhile but Thomas more or less appropriated it a year or so ago and I lost interest. Only place I could think of where we can go without being spotted. I don't believe, considering the way he used it, that Thomas ever told his mother it existed."

After another silence he asked, "Are you sure, Sam, that it was a woman you found in Thomas's room last night?"

"Positive. And it wasn't just the perfume I could smell. And she didn't leave the house. The press guy out in front would have spotted her if she'd left that way, and I watched the back entrance."

Mr. Potter sighed. "If it was Deborah, she must have wanted to get rid of the money so there would be no evidence to support my statement that Thomas was blackmailing someone."

"But why would she do that to you?" Opal asked.

Mr. Potter gave them the gist of his conversation with Wagstaff and Prudence Burkett's determination to get him out of the way. Never in his life had he talked with as little restraint as he continually found himself doing with Sam and Opal. Alien as they were from everything in his life, he felt a great deal of genuine affection for them. Curiously enough, he trusted them both, in spite of Sam's record. They both had a quality that had been conspicuously lacking for him in recent years. They were vividly alive.

"Have you known this guy Wagstaff long?" Sam asked.

"All my life. Why?"

"Because," Sam said succinctly, "it stinks. I never heard of any lawyer who wasn't a shyster advising his client to make a run for it. Even if no one had suspected you before, they would after that. And," he went on before Mr. Potter could speak, "all that stuff about being afraid to have to face a witch doctor – nuts! You aren't crazy and they know it. Anyone would know it. In fact, you're smart enough to have figured that out for yourself."

Mr. Potter made no reply. Opal caught at his arm so unexpectedly that the car was momentarily out of control.

"Oh, I'm sorry," she exclaimed. "I didn't mean to do that. Only I just thought of something. Suppose this old man knows his daughter wants to marry the guy with the halo. And the guy is the one who pushed Jennie–" the eagerness died out of her voice. "No, that's no good. No matter what she wanted, her father would hardly let her marry a killer."

189

"The one person who would stand up for Fullmer even if he were a killer is Deborah," Mr. Potter told her. "If he is the one who returned the park key this morning she will never admit it. No," he checked himself as Opal had checked her flight of fancy. "No, even for Fullmer Deborah would not cover the murder of her brother."

"Unless her brother blackmailed him. Who's side would she take then?"

"I don't know."

"We've thought of everyone except the Wagstaff girl," Sam said. "Ouch! Opal, your elbow nearly went through my ribs."

"Pat is incapable of murder," Mr. Potter said and the friendliness had faded from his voice. "I know that much about her."

"When you are in love," Opal said bluntly, "you can't see what people are like. You just feel." Before he could reply she said, "A car has followed us all the way, a blue Plymouth."

Mr. Potter stopped for a traffic light in Brewster and in the rear-view mirror saw the Plymouth close behind. The man at the wheel had a cap pulled down over his eyes.

"Hang on!" The lights turned and the convertible leaped ahead. When they had gone up the second hill there was no sign of the Plymouth and Mr. Potter turned onto a side road, dropping down to normal speed. At this season of the year, the summer houses were still unoccupied and the passage of the vivid car was unnoticed. He took a narrow lane, a second and third, and turned up a steep, rough road into the woods. He brought the car to a halt in front of a small frame cottage.

They piled out and Mr. Potter unlocked the door, flung it open and stood stock still.

"Well," Sam said at length, "either Thomas gave a party to end parties or this place has been used as testing ground for the Bomb."

The cottage consisted of a big living room, two small bedrooms, a bath and kitchen. The whole place had been torn apart. In the kitchen the contents of flour, sugar and coffee containers had been dumped on the floor and raked over. Even the mattress in the bedroom had been ripped open with a razor that had been dropped carelessly. The second bedroom had been converted into a dark room and here the destruction had been complete. Jars and bottles were broken, a filing cabinet for prints had been ransacked, two expensive cameras had been ruthlessly smashed.

This had not been just a search; the wanton destruction had been for its own sweet sake. Mr. Potter stood and looked, without speaking, without expression. Something in his very stillness kept the others silent. Murder, he was thinking. Anyone can accept murder because in his heart he is aware of hot anger and impulses that can be bridled only by strict control. But this — the feeling behind this is more dangerous; more deadly, in a paradoxical sort of way. Because it is without meaning. Hate for hate's sake.

He went back to the living room, stepped over a stack of broken records and picked up the telephone.

"Hey," Sam intervened hastily, "what are you going to do?"

"Report this to the state police."

"We're running away from the police. Remember?" Sam said.

II

At ten o'clock that night they found a motel without any cars. "Keep out of sight as far as possible," Sam suggested. "This is a speedy bus but it is conspicuous." He went inside the house where, through an unshaded window, they could see a woman seated at a table, knitting.

"He'll handle her," Opal prophesied confidently. "Don't you worry."

Mr. Potter turned to smile at her. "You like him, don't you."

Opal nodded. "I'm crazy about him but he just thinks I'm a good pal. I never in all my life saw a woman who wanted to be a good pal. I get so mad but there's nothing I can do about it."

"You could do better," Mr. Potter told her, smiling. "I like Sam but it doesn't seem to me a confidence man would make a good husband."

"If he weren't so soft and bone lazy he could be a very successful man. The trouble with Sam is that he had a hard time as a kid, worse than me. I came out of the slums but at least I had a family; Sam came out of an orphanage and he didn't have anyone. He has a lot of talents though you might not think it. Only no one ever thought he was important so he didn't care enough to make something of himself."

Sam came out with two keys. "There isn't another soul here tonight," he said in a tone of satisfaction, "and I talked so fast she forgot to ask for the license number of the car." He tossed one key to Mr. Potter. "Number three. That's for you and me. The car is parked beside the cabin, you know."

"Good." Mr. Potter turned to Opal. "You won't be nervous alone?"

"I'll look around her cabin first and see that she locks herself in," Sam promised. "Anyhow, all she has to do is yell if anything happens."

The lights in Opal's cabin soon went out and, in cabin three, Sam went to bed. Mr. Potter sat at the window in the dark, which did not prove to be good company. It was peopled with images: Jennie's body hurtling out of the sky; Thomas's eyes staring at him from the trunk of the car; himself peering between the bars of a mental institution, probably gibbering, while Deborah used his money to win Fullmer away from Pat. What had Fullmer's appointment been the night Jennie died, and how could he find out?

The door of the main house opened and Mr. Potter saw the manager of the motel come out, a flashlight in her hand. She went straight to the yellow convertible, turned the flashlight on the license and then went back. Helplessly, Mr. Potter watched her through the lighted window as she dialed a number.

He shook Sam. When the latter answered in a startled voice, he said in a low tone, "We've got to get out. The manager checked the license number and made a telephone call. There must be a general alarm out for us."

While Sam dressed, he ran across to the next cabin to awaken Opal.

Ten minutes later the convertible, with lights out, backed down the incline to the road and roared away. At the first crossroads it turned west and slowed down.

"Where do we go?" Mr. Potter asked blankly.

"I don't know." Opal was not far from tears and gallantly trying to conceal the fact.

"We could try to get over the Canadian border," Sam said tentatively.

"But running away won't solve anything." Mr. Potter considered the possibilities.

Sam laughed shortly. "We are running away."

"Actually," Mr. Potter told him in a queer voice, "we are just following instructions. Where did you say you and Jennie come from?"

"Hackers Point, Ohio. Why?"

Mr. Potter opened the glove compartment and consulted a map. "All right, we'll try Hackers Point. There is a lot I'd like to find out about Mrs. Newcomb. Someone brought her to New York and we've got to discover who it was."

He settled down to a steady fifty-five miles an hour while Opal turned sleepily and put her head on Sam's shoulder. Before long they were both asleep.

There was nothing ahead on the road, and only a few cars behind. While his two companions slept, Mr. Potter drove through the night, playing his favorite game with himself. He was no longer alone. Beside him rode Pat, a gentle Pat with the strain gone from her face. He talked to her as he had never talked to anyone in his life, unburdening his shy heart. And Pat understood.

The Pat of Mr. Potter's dreams bore little relation to the reality but that did not disturb him. The Mr. Potter of his dreams was different, too. The Pat he had conjured out of his loneliness confided to him that she thought Bernard Fullmer ridiculous, that she was weary of his vaulting ambition, that she preferred Mr. Potter. You and I, she had said after Bernard's speech. You and I.

The night seemed very short to Mr. Potter. Dawn was breaking when he crossed the Pennsylvania state line. Although he was not really worried about the cars behind him, he felt a sense of relief when a small black Ford stopped at the state line and drew up at the side of the road. A car came into the main highway and fell into place behind Mr. Potter. Much farther back, a shabby blue Plymouth followed the other car.

Chapter 13

At seven o'clock they stopped for breakfast at a roadside stand. Rain was falling heavily, blown by gusts of March wind. They were all at low ebb, tired, sleepy, depressed, and the rain that soaked them before they could run inside the diner completed their demoralization.

Mr. Potter, only half aroused from his phantom conversation with Pat, had difficulty in bringing himself back to the unpalatable reality. Opal, shivering in her inadequate coat, was groggy with sleep. Only Sam was his usual self, his eyes bright behind the round glasses, smiling and cheerful.

In the over-heated diner their wet clothes steamed. A sleepy proprietor served coffee, bacon and eggs and went back to sleep while they ate. A radio disk jockey was trying to sound cheerful, in spite of drenching rain and the early hour. He provided bright patter between records.

On the hour he broke off his synthetic jokes for five minutes of news. Because of his sleeping companions and his own preoccupation, Mr. Potter had not turned on the radio in the car all night, so the news struck him with its full impact.

The police, the voice announced cheerfully, were still investigating the murder in New York of Thomas Burkett, whose body, savagely beaten about the head, had been found in the trunk of Hiram Potter's car. Hiram Potter, heir to the Potter fortune, had disappeared and a five-state alarm had gone out for him. Railroad stations, bus lines and airports had been alerted.

Potter was believed to be in the company of a well-known confidence man and a model, Opal Reed, with whom he had been arrested in a recent raid on the Gink Club in New York City. The raid, as would be remembered, had netted three men who had taken part in a series of hotel burglaries. Listeners to the XYZ station would recall that it was also into the garden of Mr. Potter's home on Gramercy Park that a young girl had fallen to her death a few days before. At that time, no connection had been established between the girl and Hiram Potter.

The girl's stepmother had identified her as

Jennie Newcomb of Hackers Point. Her father, Frank Newcomb, had been well known in eastern Ohio where he was still remembered. His garage was now owned by Joe Weldon. Mrs. Newcomb had believed Jennie's death to be suicide but the police had ascertained that Jennie and the model, Opal Reed, had been roommates. Apparently, Mr. Potter had some knowledge of the girl although he had not admitted any acquaintance with her and had failed to identify her when her body was found.

Mrs. Prudence Burkett, aunt of the missing millionaire, declared in an interview last night that she thought poor Hiram had lost his mind and that he was not responsible for his actions. "I cannot believe," she stated, "that Hiram would brutally murder my beloved son if he were in his right mind. Since his mother's death his actions have become incomprehensible. He has been drinking heavily, associating with undesirable people, and threatened to turn me out of this house without a penny." Miss Burkett, cousin of the missing man, said that on the night of her brother's disappearance and murder, young Potter quarreled violently with him, and uttered threats against both her mother and herself.

"Potter," went on the cheerful voice which Mr. Potter was beginning to loathe, "is twenty-eight years old, five feet ten, with fair hair and blue eyes. When last seen he wore a dark gray suit with a narrow pin stripe and a mourning band around the left sleeve, a navy blue neck-tie, a dark overcoat and soft gray hat. He was driving a yellow convertible with a black top and the license number NY 13579. Anyone seeing this man or the car will please notify the police at once. Remember — this man may be dangerous."

Three pairs of eyes shifted automatically toward the sleeping counter man. Mr. Potter left money for their breakfast and they went quietly out into the rain.

They drove on, the car jarred now and then by the impact of the wind. Even the windshield wipers could not keep the glass clear because of the steam from their wet clothing. Sam leaned forward and wiped it with his handkerchief.

"Associating with undesirable people," Opal said at last. "That's us, Sam."

"Look out," he warned her. "Don't make Hiram mad. This man may be dangerous."

Mr. Potter said nothing at all.

By mid-morning they reached Hackers Point, the small Ohio town in which Jennie Newcomb and Sam Trumble had spent their childhood. It was an average middle western small town without signs of extreme wealth or extreme poverty; with a huge parking lot for employees' cars outside the main factory; with television antennae over the roofs of the homes and a space for the family automobile. Not a beautiful town nor an old one, but people lived here with a degree of comfort that existed no place else in the world.

Mr. Potter crawled along Main Street, which was equipped with the usual churches, supermarkets, drugstores, five and tens, uneasily aware that people turned for a second look at the yellow convertible. Sam shared his uneasiness.

"The first thing we've got to do is put your car out of sight. I know a good place."

The place Sam had in mind was a ramshackle barn about a half mile beyond Hackers Point. Mr. Potter drove the convertible inside with a sigh of relief. The barn was cold, dark and damp. Here and there, puddles stood on the dirt floor from water dripping down from the leaky roof. He turned his collar up around his neck and shivered, yawning widely.

"What do we do now?" he asked.

"You get some sleep," Opal said promptly. "Sam and I slept most of the night but you haven't had any rest at all."

The back seat was narrow and Mr. Potter

looked at it dubiously. Then he stumbled out of the car and spread the lap rug over the hay, which was only a couple of feet thick, damp and sour smelling. But he was too tired to care. He lay down, wrapping his overcoat around him. With a piece of sour hay tickling his nose and a rat scampering out of sight, he turned on his side and fell asleep.

Opal and Sam sat in the car. "What do we do now," she asked. "We're in an awful spot. We can't stay here indefinitely. If we go out we'll be arrested for murder. After that broadcast, we can't even go anywhere for food."

Sam polished his glasses. "I don't know what we can do," he admitted. "A good seventy-five per cent of the people in Hackers Point know me by sight. That lets me out."

"So it's up to me," Opal said thoughtfully. "But there have been a lot of pictures of me, too."

"They didn't attract much attention to your face, sugar," Sam pointed out.

Opal studied herself critically in the rear-view mirror. Then she combed her hair back, wiped off the mascara and eye shadow and most of the lipstick. She took the scarf from around her neck and tied it over her head. With a grimace she turned to Sam.

He said the proper thing. "Never saw you look so nice." Oddly enough, it was true. Without the widened lips her mouth was full and warm and sweet. Without the mascara her eyes were candid and direct.

Mr. Potter muttered under his breath and turned restlessly. Opal looked at him and smiled. "He's really sweet. And attractive when he smiles. Have you noticed? It starts with a kind of twinkle in his eyes before it touches his mouth. And he hasn't panicked once. He's figuring things out as cool as a cucumber."

"Don't let me see you falling for him," Sam warned her with a laugh and Opal gave him a quick, questioning look and then turned away from him. Sam sobered. "He has guts. I'll say that for him. All the cards stacked against us and he doesn't fall out of the game. He starts figuring his chances and deals another hand. His own family is trying to do him dirt and as for his lawyer – no matter what Potter thinks, I believe that guy is covering for the would-be-son-in-law of his."

"Well," Opal said on a shaky breath, "what do I do?"

"Sure you want to try?" She looked so young and vulnerable that Sam felt a sudden pang at letting her go alone and cursed his own helplessness.

She nodded and managed a smile. "Yes, I'm sure."

"You aren't scared?"

"Of course I'm scared. But when I think of someone pushing Jennie, and her stepmother saying they didn't, and the police thinking you and Hiram killed that cousin of his—"

Sam put his arm around her and patted her shoulder in a brotherly way which annoyed Opal. "Mrs. Newcomb took all the money out of her husband's garage and put it into a dough-nut shop on Taft Street. Taft runs at right angles to Main, there's a beauty parlor on the corner and the doughnut shop is right next door. There's a blue awning. You can't miss it."

Opal nodded. "I'll find it."

"Don't be scared, honey. Mrs. Newcomb didn't get a look at you at the morgue. You told me so yourself. And the only pictures she has seen of you are — well — disturbing."

Opal looked up hopefully and he grinned companionably at her. She looked away. Sometimes, she thought, a girl might as well give up.

"Mrs. Newcomb has a kink about money," Sam went on. "She doesn't believe in banks so she keeps the stuff in the house, lives in an annex behind the shop and she's got more bolts and locks and burglar alarms than they have at Tiffany's."

"I'm not afraid of going there," Opal said dubiously, "at least not so very afraid. But I don't know how I'm going to get the truth out of her about Jennie."

"Don't try," Sam advised her. "Look the place over and see what you think of her. It's about all you can do. And at least you might be able to buy some doughnuts. It's going to be a long time between meals with our present set-up."

Opal took a long breath. "Well, here we go." She got out of the car, pulled the scarf around her head, turned up her coat collar and plunged out into the drenching rain. The road was muddy, the wind tugged at her coat and scarf, the rain beat on her face. She slogged grimly through the mud, feeling the water squeeze between her toes when her shoes were soaked. A wet strand of hair hung damply against her cheek.

There was no one on the road, not a car passed her during the half-mile walk. Hackers Point was a relief because at least there were sidewalks instead of gummy mud. Main Street was rain swept and almost deserted. Opal found the beauty parlor, caught sight of her reflection and winced. At least no one would take her for a glamorous model.

She ducked under the blue canopy and entered the doughnut shop, which was warm, dry and brightly lighted. On one side doughnuts turned in a machine, at a sparklingly clean counter golden brown doughnuts were piled on plates or stacked in boxes. There were two small white tables.

Opal dripped her way to one of the tables and sat down, taking off her wet scarf. A plain girl with a bad complexion smiled at her. "Some day!" she said.

Mrs. Newcomb was not in the shop and the door to the annex was closed. Opal ordered coffee and doughnuts. She looked ruefully at the muddy prints of her shoes on the immaculate floor. "I'm so sorry. I've messed the place up."

"Boy, are you wet!" the waitress said. "Better let me hang up that coat or it will be too wrinkled to wear. Anyhow, you'll catch cold sitting in wet clothes."

Considering that she had been wearing wet clothes for nearly five hours Opal thought she would have to take her chance, although she gratefully relinquished the coat to the friendly waitress, spread her scarf over the other chair, and drank some of the hot coffee.

"Better take those shoes off, too," the girl said. "They're soaking." She put them down beside the hissing radiator.

"I'm being an awful nuisance," Opal said.

"Wednesday's early closing day and it just struck twelve. No one else will be in. How'd you ever get so wet?"

"I'm visiting friends in the country," Opal said, and went on to describe starting to town, a flat tire, how she had walked on, not realizing how far it was. She made it so vivid that she almost believed it herself. She drank the hot coffee gratefully and ate the doughnuts.

There was no sign of Mrs. Newcomb and she began to wonder whether the woman had ever returned from New York. She re-ordered, puzzled about how to broach the subject of Jennie.

"This is a sweet little shop," she remarked.

"You ain't seen nothin'. The boss is going to expand. That's where she is now, seeing about a lease for the building next door. She wants to put in a regular restaurant."

"I shouldn't think anyone could make that much money out of doughnuts," Opal remarked. "A girl I met in New York told me her stepmother had a doughnut shop here but I don't think she was making much money."

"You come from New York?" the girl asked enviously. "That must have been Jennie. This is the only doughnut shop in Hackers Point."

"Yes, her name was Jennie Newcomb. Did you know her?"

"Same class at school and she was my best girl friend. A terrible thing happened to her."

"I saw it in the papers the other day," Opal said and could not control a shiver.

"Mrs. Newcomb hadn't ought to have let her go to the city alone, she was so young and had no friends there or anything, but I guess she was just glad to get rid of the kid. Afraid she'd expect part of the earnings of the shop. Though it was bought with her own dead father's money and he was fond of Jennie; wanted to look after her because she was so sort of — you know."

Opal nodded.

"But he was no match for the boss. Nobody's a match for the boss," the waitress added bitterly.

"How'd she ever know it was Jennie who died?" Opal asked.

"She saw her body in the morgue."

"But how," Opal hesitated and then went on, "how did she happen to go to the morgue? What made her think it might be Jennie?"

"I don't know. I come to work and there was a note saying the boss would be gone for a couple of days. But it wasn't true — what she said about suicide—" the waitress broke off. "There she comes now."

"I liked Jennie," Opal said quickly. "Can't you meet me somewhere and tell me about her?"

"Public library in half an hour," the waitress said.

Opal slid her wet feet into the wetter shoes, put on her coat and was tying the scarf around her head when Mrs. Newcomb came in. She was bigger than Opal had remembered, the biggest woman she had ever seen outside a circus. Her eyes brushed over Opal, fell on the muddy tracks of her shoes.

"Bess," Mrs. Newcomb said sharply, "get a mop and clean up this mess."

"Yes, Mrs. Newcomb."

Opal bought five boxes of doughnuts to placate Mrs. Newcomb. The fat woman watched the money drop into the cash register. Queer, Opal thought, I could almost feel each coin in my own fingers. Then, avoiding the woman as far as possible, not an easy feat in the small shop, she went out into the rain, the boxes of doughnuts tucked under her arm.

The library, an old brown frame house, was beyond the church on Main Street, and Opal settled herself in the reading room. Aside from the librarian who was working at her desk and a couple of small boys discussing books on aviation, the building was deserted. Opal hung her coat over a chair near the radiator, tucked her shoes under it, and sat as close to it as she could, shivering and sneezing.

She picked up a copy of *Vogue* from a table, opened it on her lap, and tried to rub her hair dry with a handkerchief. While her shoes steamed and the radiator thumped and water dripped off her coat, her eyes rested on photographs of improbable women wearing mink coats and diamonds. She was not much given to thinking but she was busy now, considering what Bess had told her. Mrs. Newcomb had suddenly acquired enough money to rent the building next door and install a restaurant. Only how could they find out where she had got the money? That was a job for the police and they dared not call in the police. Anyhow, Opal admitted to herself, she would not have the courage to tackle Mrs. Newcomb. She was afraid of her.

A man in a transparent raincoat came into the reading room, picked up a copy of the *Hackers Point Sentinel* and settled down to scan its pages. Opal looked at him swiftly. Why, she wondered in surprise, was so good looking a man wasting his time reading. He did not look at her at all.

She shook her coat so that it sent off a shower of little drops that fell on the newspaper.

"I'm so sorry," she said.

He looked up and smiled. He had a nice smile. A lot handsomer than most men she'd sighed over in the movies. "Not at all," he replied vaguely.

Opal wondered in some alarm what had happened to her looks. She rubbed her wet feet together and under the table. She was beginning to get warm. The coffee had helped. And though her wet clothes were giving the library the atmosphere of a steam laundry no one seemed to mind.

She turned a page of *Vogue* and became absorbed in an article that explained that one should plan a dinner menu so there would be no tiresome recurrence of color; the problem and chief drawback of French chefs, she read, fascinated, was that they had no color sense in meal-planning.

There was a smell of wet rubber and the waitress came in, took off a crackling raincoat with a hood and, after a wistful glance at the good-looking man who was absorbed in the *Sentinel,* having now reached the page devoted to women's clubs, she pulled up a chair close to Opal.

"Sorry to keep you waiting," she said in a sibilant carrying whisper, "but Mrs. Newcomb was in an awful mood and I had to scrub the whole floor. I told her I was going to quit. Anyhow, there's an opening at the soda fountain in the drugstore and it would be livelier. Kids coming in after school and no one to jump down your throat every minute. No wonder

Jennie left home. I don't know how she ever stood it, but I miss her. She was my best friend."

Opal found it easy to understand the bond between these two unattractive, defenseless girls. "She was sweet," she said. "That's why I don't see how anyone could have treated her so mean she'd commit suicide."

"She never. That's what I wanted to tell you. She never." The waitress fumbled in her handbag and pulled out a crumpled envelope. "That's her last letter, only three weeks ago. I never got time to answer it. I wisht I'd answered it. Look, you can read it if you want."

Opal opened the letter in Jennie's familiar, unformed scrawl. "New York is exciting," she had written. "You have no idea. I don't ever want to leave it. I guess I've never been this happy before. Everything worked out in the most marvelous way. I finally found Sam Trumble — you remember Sam — and he was just as nice as he used to be, no matter what some people say, and he helped me find a room with the nicest girl. You'd be crazy about her. And simply beautiful, like on the magazines." Opal tried to swallow the lump in her throat.

"And I finally got a job — forty-five dollars a week!! — can you believe it? Me making forty-five dollars a week? And I got it the queerest way. One day I was following up ads for a job and got tired. Standing in line is the awfulest thing and then they just look at you as if you were a bolt of cloth or something — and I was way downtown so I went to Battery Park and sat down on a bench to rest my feet.

"This man sat down beside me and began to talk. A perfect gentleman, you could see that at once. And he was looking for a stenographer, didn't care about experience. What he wanted was a trustworthy girl. So I told him all about myself.

"You could see it was all right. So I got the job and then I started working in an office and then this man got to be my boss and he's wonderful.

"Do try to save your money so you won't have to work for my stepmother any more and you can come to New York. Even if you don't have any dates at first, and I haven't yet, you won't be lonely. There's so much to see. Loads of love, Jennie."

"I'd like to show this to someone who thinks Jennie killed herself over a man. May I borrow it?"

"You can keep it," Bess said. "But I wisht I'd got to answer her, though."

Opal put on her shoes, slid her arms into the soggy coat and tied the scarf over her head. "Which way are you going?" she asked, putting

213

her letter in her handbag and reaching for the boxes of doughnuts.

Bess looked embarrassed. "I'm going to stay and get a book."

The two girls parted, Bess going toward the stacks, Opal toward the street and the rain.

The big man folded the newspaper neatly and picked up his raincoat. By the time he went down the steps of the library, Opal was walking swiftly along the street. He watched her for a moment and then got into a shabby blue Plymouth that had been parked outside the library. He slid away from the curb, taking the same direction.

Chapter 14

Mr. Potter pulled out a straw from under his wilted collar and scrambled to his feet. A stubble of beard made him look mildly disreputable; his suit, wrinkled and stained from the damp hay, betrayed the fact that it had been slept in. He groaned as he attempted to straighten his back.

"I'm too old for this sort of thing," he complained. He took one of the doughnuts Opal handed him, bit into it and tossed it away. "And too hungry for that sort of thing! How many doughnuts have we eaten today?"

"Four dozen," Opal said. "I'm a little tired of them myself. But we don't dare take a risk of going to any restaurant around here." She added glumly, "Around anywhere. I must say I never expected to be one of those people whose pictures are in postoffices, with numbers and fingerprints and things: 'This Woman Wanted.'"

She and Sam were seated in the car. The broken barn door had been partly closed and the car lights were on. They dared not keep the motor running for the heater because they could not run the risk of lowering the supply of gas. The barn was cold and dark and damp, although the rain had stopped.

Mr. Potter shook straw off his overcoat, slipped it on and started out of the barn.

"Where are you going?" Opal asked, alarmed by his air of grim determination.

"I'm going to get us something fit to eat," Mr. Potter said calmly.

"But you'll be recognized!" As he shrugged, she implored, "Sam, don't let him go!"

Sam exchanged looks with Mr. Potter and grinned at her. "Unless I knock him out I don't know how I'd stop him, sugar." He shook his head. "You may not have realized it, but this guy has a will of his own."

Mr. Potter tossed the car key to Sam. "If anyone should bother you before I get back, you two had better cut and run."

He switched on a flashlight and went into the night. He had no destination in mind. He simply knew that he was hungry and that he had to have food. Here and there he passed a farmhouse and worked his way as close to it as possible. At one kitchen door he stopped, his nostrils flaring while he inhaled the smells of cornbeef and cabbage, never before a favorite dish of his. But, as the family had gathered around the kitchen table, he saw no way of getting their dinner without fighting them all single handed. In his desperation, he did not immediately relinquish even this idea, but when he looked more closely and saw that there were at least four hefty young men gathered around the table, he made off.

About a quarter of a mile from the barn, he was attracted by the sight of half a dozen cars drawn to the side of the road. On the hillside was a new ranch house ablaze with light. A dinner party, he thought. Just what the doctor ordered. He pulled his collar up around his face, his hat brim down over his eyes, and started toward the house, keeping out of the light that poured from the picture windows.

He bumped against an obstruction, cautiously flashed on his light and read the cheering words: BEWARE — WATCH DOG. As an indication that this was no bluff there was a deep baying bark and a dog came leaping down the hill toward him. Mr. Potter stood motionless. The dog checked its plunge and stood barking.

"Why, old friend, what's all this?" Mr. Potter said. The barking stopped. The animal was near enough for Mr. Potter to see a German shepherd, its hair standing up in a ruff around its neck. "Bad night for you to be out, old fellow," Mr. Potter said sympathetically. "It's a shame." His hand hung quiet at his side. He was careful not to budge.

The dog growled once, low in its throat, and moved forward. It snuffed at Mr. Potter's hand, getting acquainted. There was no fear in the man who spoke again. A wet muzzle explored his hand. Then the hand moved, touched the dog's head, scratched it slowly.

"That's better. Come on. You'll be more likely to trust me if you go along."

They walked up through a rough field, the ground still frozen, crossed the gravel driveway cautiously, moved around to the side of the house. Through the picture window Mr. Potter could see a dozen people drinking cocktails in front of a blazing fire. He crept slowly around the house toward the kitchen, now and then speaking softly to the dog, his hand touching it in a companionable way.

The kitchen was brightly lighted. Only one person was there, a harrassed young woman in a dinner dress covered by an apron. She took off the apron, slung it over a chair, picked up a platter of appetizers and went through a swinging door. Mr. Potter turned the doorknob softly and went into the kitchen, the police dog padding at his side.

He looked around in disapproval. A picnic supper, that's all it was. He hoped virtuously that the woman's husband would divorce her. Hot dogs floated in a pan of boiling water. Baked beans stood in an open can. He considered the baked beans and then lifted his head, sniffing. There was a kettle of onion soup on the stove. Things were picking up.

Through the swing door there came a burst of laughter as someone finished a story and Mr. Potter stood stock still. But the door did not move. He picked up the kettle of soup and the opened can of unheated beans. Then he turned, his head cocked on one side, studying in amusement the dog which was snuffing much as he himself had done, blackmailing him with imploring looks.

"A gentleman con man, that's what you are." He took a broken frankfurter out of a sink strainer and held it out to the dog, laying a five-dollar bill as conspicuously as possible on the table.

With the soup kettle in one hand and the beans in the other he sidled through the doorway and the dog came with him. Quietly he retraced his steps to the road. There he ordered the dog back but it had given its heart and refused to leave its new master.

With an anxious look around — you never know where you'll encounter thieves, Mr. Potter thought indignantly — he set down his loot, took the dog back and let it into the kitchen.

The clouds were parting and the moon looked palely from behind a thin white veil when Mr. Potter reached the barn and put down his supper. Sam Trumble looked from the soup kettle to Mr. Potter's triumphant face and laughed until he rolled in the straw. Then they squatted on the ground around the kettle and practiced the difficult art of drinking from it. The beans they ate with their fingers, dipping into the can in a way that Mr. Potter assured them had been practiced by their ancestors, if one could go back enough centuries. He apologized gravely for providing no silverware. They ate until nothing was left. And all the time Sam laughed.

When they had finished, Opal threw her arms around Mr. Potter and kissed him exuberantly. "Hiram," she declared, "I love you."

"That's not a full heart speaking," Sam warned him. "It's a full stomach."

"The least I owed you was a meal," Mr. Potter said. "I've taken the two of you off, got you suspected of murder, let Opal sit around all day in wet clothing, and I haven't so much as provided food and shelter." Absently, he pulled a straw out from under his collar. "Well," he said decisively, "we can't stop here. Opal will have pneumonia. Let's get going."

They piled into the car and Sam said, "Where now?"

"Sooner or later," Mr. Potter promised rashly, "I'll find a place where you can sleep, warm and dry."

"Mm," Opal breathed. "That's heaven you are describing."

"But first," Mr. Potter said, "we haven't really accomplished anything at Hackers Point that we set out to do. Oh, thanks to Opal, we've got evidence that Mrs. Newcomb lied about Jennie, and that the woman has picked up a sizable sum of money recently. But who gave it to her? And who told her Jennie was dead and made her come to New York to identify the body and tell that suicide story?"

"Mrs. Newcomb is a magpie," Sam said slowly. "She always was. Even when I was a kid. One summer I worked at Newcomb's garage and she'd come around, picking up every blessed thing that was loose, pieces of string, bits of paper. If there's any evidence, she wouldn't destroy it because that would be against her nature. Even if it were dangerous and she knew it. The compulsion is too strong."

"So?" Mr. Potter asked.

"So," Sam suggested, peering through his

221

glasses in a questioning way at the other man, "I'm going to take a look. It's ten-thirty now and the old girl probably goes to bed about ten o'clock."

"If you get caught breaking in," Opal wailed, "you'll be arrested."

"If we don't do something drastic pretty darned soon," Sam pointed out, "we'll all be arrested. Can you think of a better plan?"

Opal couldn't.

"Then I'm going to try. I'll be back as soon as I can make it."

"We'll all go," Mr. Potter decided. "There's no point in staying here. Another twelve hours and we'll be covered with mildew."

As the car moved slowly along the road to Hackers Point he heard Opal glumly humming the Prisoners Song.

II

As the convertible approached the corner of First Street and Taft, a green Chevrolet rocketed down Taft and made a left turn on two wheels. Mr. Potter jammed on his brakes and brought his car to a stop.

"If this bus didn't stop on a dime," Sam said, "we'd have been hit head-on. What's the matter with that fool?"

"We might as well park here," Mr. Potter said. "Opal, can you drive?"

"No."

He put on parking lights and left the motor running. "Keep your eyes open. If anything bothers you, sound the horn. Fortunately, there aren't many of these two-toned jobs around." He got out of the car and heard the door on the opposite side slam. In a moment Sam joined him.

Hackers Point had gone to bed. Aside from the movie house and the drugstore there were few lights. The doughnut shop was dark. Even to protect her cash register, Mrs. Newcomb could not bring herself to leave a night light burning, eating away pennies.

The two men went down the alley back of Taft Street. An addition had been built onto the back of the doughnut shop, which Mrs. Newcomb used as her living quarters, and a board fence enclosed it.

Mr. Potter stretched out his hand and Sam quickly brushed it aside. "Wait a minute," he whispered. "Let me see." He shaded the flashlight and examined the fence. "I thought so. It's electrified. See that wire strung along the top?"

"We'll have to be more careful, that's all."

223

Mr. Potter spoke close to his ear. Then he rested his hands on the cross-brace and vaulted over without touching the wire. "Come on," he whispered. "It's easy. Just be careful that you clear the wire."

In a moment Sam landed with a thump beside him. They stood looking at the annex. Cautiously Sam tried the back door but it was securely locked. He crept toward the open bedroom window and listened. There was not a sound.

He stole back to Mr. Potter. "I can't hear her breathing. She may not be asleep yet."

"How about the other window?"

Sam tried it and came back to report that it was locked.

Mr. Potter sighed. "Then we'll simply have to get in the bedroom." He took hold of the sill and pulled himself up until his head and shoulders were above it. The room was completely still. It felt empty. He raised himself up on the sill, cautiously parted the curtains and let himself down soundlessly in the room. He shaded the flashlight and looked around. There was no one in the room, although the covers had been tossed back and someone had been in the bed.

He leaned out and spoke softly to Sam who scrambled in after him.

"She's probably in the bathroom," he whispered. "She—" The flashlight touched a heap of clothes on the floor, touched gray hair, paused.

"Oh, my God," Sam said. "Oh, my God. Oh my—"

"Shut up!" Mr. Potter leaned against the wall, fighting back nausea. Then he turned the flashlight full on the swollen, distorted face, the eyes bulging in their pockets of flesh, the tongue thrust out at them grotesquely. A rope was embedded in the rolls of fat of Mrs. Newcomb's neck with a stick twisted in it to tighten the rope. She was dead. With a shudder of distaste Mr. Potter touched the revolting face. It was still warm. Then he remembered the green Chevrolet that had gone rocketing around the corner at such terrific speed.

"She's been dead only a few minutes," he said in his usual tone and Sam was startled. "We won't wake her. And we've got to work fast. If we are caught here now it will be the end of us."

Skirting the body that lay like an obscene lump on the floor, they searched the room, the desk, the dresser and clothes closet. Sam looked behind a picture on the wall and finally turned a chair upside down. He gave a muffled exclamation and caught himself looking at the dead woman to see whether she had been aroused. Taped to the bottom of the chair was a stack of currency. Ignoring Mr. Potter's protests, he ripped away the tape and counted the money.

"Twenty-five hundred dollars," he said. "It seems to be a one-price outfit."

"Put the money back where you found it," Mr. Potter said sharply. "Any letters?"

There was nothing else.

"Then let's get out of here. We're too late to find out what Mrs. Newcomb knew."

"Just a minute," Sam said. "I'll try the shop."

"Don't be a complete fool. We've got to move fast."

"She might keep something there just because it seems like an unlikely place," Sam insisted.

"We can't take the chance. Come on." Mr. Potter was in a fever to get away, to leave behind him the dead woman with the horrible face. Three dead bodies and only a suspicion as to the identity of the murderer who was riding madly toward New York behind the wheel of the green Chevrolet.

Sam ignored him, opened the door to the shop and disappeared. Down the street came the mellow sound of a two-toned horn. Someone flung open the outside door of the doughnut shop. Evidently the murderer had left it ajar in his haste. Mr. Potter heard an exclamation from the shop and, scrambling out of the bedroom window, vaulted over the fence and raced down the alley.

"I was afraid you wouldn't hear," Opal said in relief as he got in the car. "There's a patrolman trying the shop door on his rounds. Where's Sam?"

"He caught Sam." Mr. Potter peered forward, ignoring Opal's smothered cry. He started the car, turned the corner cruising toward the doughnut shop. It was brightly lighted now. Inside Sam stood arguing with a patrolman.

"I've warned him and warned him," Opal choked. "What can we do now?"

"Collect him, of course." Mr. Potter was surprised.

"You can't do that."

"We have to do it," he said patiently. "Mrs. Newcomb has been strangled."

"Dead?"

"Very."

"Oh, my God!"

"Don't lose your nerve now, Opal. Hold the door open, will you?"

A police car was coming from the opposite direction. It pulled up across the street and an officer got out and crossed the street to the lighted shop, leaving one man in the driver's seat.

Inside the shop Sam had moved casually toward the door. The officer from the prowl car came in, spoke to the patrolman.

Mr. Potter touched the two-toned horn and saw Sam's head jerk toward the door. "All right," Mr. Potter said crisply.

Sam leaped for the door and raced for the convertible. Mr. Potter shot off while Opal was still dragging him inside. Behind them came a revolver shot, then another and another. The prowl car lost valuable time turning around. The convertible was moving at seventy, eighty-five, a hundred miles an hour. On the main highway the speedometer crept up to a hundred and twenty.

"You've gone crazy," Sam said, his breath coming in heavy sobbing gusts. "This is the main highway east. They'll set up blockades. We've got to head for the Canadian border."

"Nonsense," Mr. Potter said crisply. "We're going back."

"But why, for God's sake?"

"Because the murderer came from New York and has to return to New York. There's no point in silencing Mrs. Newcomb unless he turns up where he belongs."

"You haven't more than one chance in a

hundred of getting away with this," Sam warned him.

"That's a reasonable percentage. Hang on, boys and girls!"

Chapter 15

Ahead of them, there were bright neon lights and several trucks parked outside a diner. Mr. Potter expelled a sigh of relief, left the highway and eased the convertible over a rough field behind the diner. He switched off the motor and the lights.

"We can't stay here," Sam said on a note of horror.

Mr. Potter pointed to the gas indicator. It registered empty. "We can't go on. All that's been worrying me was that we would run out of gas before we found a good place to stop."

"That's all that's been worrying you, is it? I suppose," Sam said sarcastically, "this is a good place."

"Couldn't be better," Mr. Potter assured him cheerfully. "Kills two birds with one stone."

"But which birds?" Sam demanded.

Mr. Potter laughed for the first time that

night. Since the discovery of Mrs. Newcomb's body, Sam had been in a somber mood and Opal had been silent, although both men could feel her shaking as she sat between them. Mr. Potter had been grim and unapproachable.

"Well," he said now, "we have to leave the car. As a matter of fact, the sooner we get rid of it the better for us. The license number has been broadcast. As a matter of fact, it seems odd to me that we haven't been picked up before now. I don't understand it. Almost as though they were leaving us free for some reason of their own. In any case, we can't take the risk of buying gas. So—"

"So what do we do now?"

"We conceal the car back here in the dark. The chances are that, except by sheer accident, it won't be discovered until morning. And we hitch a ride to New York. I've been noticing these diners as we go along. Truck drivers stop for coffee." He slid out from under the wheel. "When I whistle you come running."

Opal opened her lips to protest but a quiet confidence in Mr. Potter's face checked her. He sauntered around in front of the diner and peered through the window. Three truck drivers were arguing about a recent decision on a prize fight. He bent down, rubbed dirt on his face, rumpled his hair, loosened his tie, opened the

231

door and limped up to the counter. In an unsteady voice he ordered coffee. His hand shook perceptibly as he raised the cup and he set it down with exaggerated care, taking his head in his hands.

"You sick?" the counter man asked him.

Mr. Potter blinked at him dazedly. "Just dizzy. I was in that accident down the road and the fools sent only one ambulance. Took my mother and my sister to the hospital but they had no room for me." He clutched his head again. "I'm not hurt, just shock, I guess, but I have a big appointment tomorrow and how the hell am I to get any transportation from here?" He took out a fat billfold and left it lying open while he paid for the coffee.

"Which way you going, Bud?" one of the truck drivers asked him.

"East."

"Too bad," he said regretfully. "I'm headed for Cleveland."

Two of the men started to drift out. The third lingered. "I'm going to Jersey City," he remarked casually to the counter man. "Trucking a load of bolts. Against the rules to carry passengers." He moved slowly. Mr. Potter's billfold fell to the floor, a twenty dollar bill fluttered down beside it. The truck driver leaned over, handed Mr. Potter the billfold, palmed the twenty.

He went out of the diner without comment and the counter man winked at Mr. Potter. "Wouldn't do to break the law," he said grinning.

Mr. Potter drifted out in the wake of the truck driver who was opening the side door. He left it open and went around in front to get behind the wheel. Whistling, Mr. Potter approached the truck. The motor started with a roar. Running feet came around the side of the diner. Mr. Potter held the door politely for Opal and Sam, climbed in behind them. The truck started.

"Where are we going?" Opal whispered.

"Jersey City."

"Ouch," Sam said. "What am I sitting on?"

"Crates of bolts."

"Feels like the rack."

"You get some sleep," Mr. Potter said. "I slept most of the day."

Propped against the boxes of bolts, which seemed all sharp edges, they made themselves as comfortable as possible. Opal and Sam fell asleep and this night, like the night before, Mr. Potter kept watch through the darkness. But this time he did not have Pat for company. He looked from Jennie's broken body to Thomas's mangled head to Mrs. Newcomb's swollen face, projecting tongue and bulging eyes. It was nightmare. Something indescribably savage had been let loose, something that was moving east ahead of them on the road like a thunderbolt.

There was no sound but the rumble of the truck. Then, after hours that were like a drug, the traffic noises gradually increased, horns sounded, and at last they were moving through the cacophony of Jersey City traffic.

It was eight o'clock in the morning when the truck jolted to a stop. "Last stop, Bud," the driver said in a low tone outside the door. "I'm going to get me some breakfast. Get out as quietly as you can or I'll be in trouble. Now's a good time. So long."

His steps moved away and Mr. Potter opened the door. They were parked on a back street in Jersey City near Journal Square. At the moment the street was nearly empty and there was no one near the truck.

They got out quietly and moved away.

"What I could do with a cup of coffee!" Opal said.

"We'd better separate for breakfast," Mr. Potter told her. "It won't do for the three of us to be seen together. Let's meet at the tubes in thirty minutes."

He stopped at a newsstand for papers, went

into a one-arm cafeteria, where people would be too busy to notice him and he could escape the attention, however casual, of a waitress. While he drank his coffee he opened the first paper. From the front page his own face looked back at him.

"Homicidal maniac loose," read the mocking headline.

He spread the paper wider, crouching behind it. Hiram Potter, he read, was leaving a trail of corpses: his cousin Thomas Burkett's brutal murder had been followed last night by the strangling of Mrs. Frank Newcomb in Hackers Point, Ohio. The widow, whose stepdaughter, Jennie Newcomb, had fallen or been pushed from an office building on Fourth Avenue...

Mr. Potter was badly shaken by the time he had gone through the papers. Why he was being accused of Mrs. Newcomb's murder he could not imagine. But that made it all the stranger that he had been allowed to drive so far in so conspicuous a car, unmolested by the police. Luck? Well, maybe. None the less, he found it disturbing. Remembering the quiet efficiency of the police the night he had reported the discovery of Thomas's body, he found it difficult to believe that, with so little effort to cover his tracks, he had remained unobserved during the past eventful hours.

As he walked toward the tube station he had to exercise self-control to keep from looking over his shoulder, and he shied like a nervous horse when he passed a policeman on traffic duty. The station was jammed with office workers and early shoppers going to Manhattan. He saw Sam, glasses gleaming, briefcase in hand, stop at the change booth. There was a folded newspaper under his arm. He glanced at Mr. Potter without recognition, brushed against him, whispering, "Follow Opal. She knows where we can go."

In a few minutes Opal appeared in the crowd. The red corduroy coat was conspicuous, Mr. Potter noticed uneasily. She dropped coins in the turnstile and went through. Sam let a couple of people follow her and then went after her. Mr. Potter went through the next turnstile and along the platform. Opal got a seat on the train; Sam stood against the middle door, his paper open to conceal his face; farther along the car, Mr. Potter hung on to a strap.

When Opal pushed her way off the subway at a downtown station Sam followed and Mr. Potter waited until the doors started to close before darting out onto the platform. He could see the red coat as Opal went up the stairs. When he got out on the street, Sam was a dozen yards ahead and Opal was turning a corner.

For a quarter of an hour she set the pace, walking briskly. Mr. Potter followed Sam, paying little attention to their direction until a street sign made him pause for a double take. They were on the Bowery. At length he saw Sam come to a halt and he bent over to retie his shoe lace. Opal had disappeared and Sam, with a swift glance around him, was opening the side door of an old church. He went inside. Mr. Potter straightened, looked to right and left, and went toward the church door.

Inside, the building was almost dark. Beyond folding doors there came a soft gleam of rose and purple and yellow as daylight filtered through stained glass windows. Sam and Opal were waiting for him.

"Come on," Opal said in a tone hushed in respect for the church, rather than because there was any danger of being heard. "There's a tiny apartment upstairs, just under the bell tower. A friend of mine lived here once when she was out of work. The pastor keeps it for people in need, and if we aren't in need now, no one ever was."

She led the way up a circular staircase that grew narrower and steeper until it was difficult to maintain footing. There was only one door on the top floor, with a mat outside. Opal felt under the mat and triumphantly held up the key.

The apartment consisted of one room with a tiny bath and an electric plate by way of a stove. She sank down on the side of the cot with a deep sigh.

"Well!" she said.

"Well?" Sam asked.

"Well," Mr. Potter assured them.

II

Opal turned away from the mirror. The reflection should have satisfied her. It should have satisfied any girl. Obviously, it gave considerable pleasure to the two young men who watched her. She saw their eyes and smiled with frank delight in their admiration.

"Just the same," she said, as though they had spoken, "I can't go around like this. What with Hiram's yellow convertible and my red coat, we might as well wear neon signs, 'Here we are; come and get us.'"

"I don't like to be an alarmist," Sam said, polishing his glasses thoughtfully. "But I must say it looks to me as though we had walked right into a trap. Our descriptions have been broadcast, we need clothes, we don't dare go out for food. We're caught, as Dorothy Parker put it, like a trap in a trap."

Mr. Potter regarded his own disheveled reflection. He rubbed a hand over his unshaven jaw. "I must say," he declared with some complacency, "I begin to look more in character." Seeing the dejected expression of his companions, he added, "I've got an idea."

"Every time you've had an idea," Sam said gloomily, "we've ended by having to run."

"I'm going home," Mr. Potter explained. There, he told them, he could replenish not only his own wardrobe and Sam's as well, but he could raid Deborah's closet for clothes for Opal. "And no one," he assured her, "would look at you twice in Deborah's clothes. You'd be practically invisible."

Sam did not bother to answer. He simply spread out a newspaper before Mr. Potter. There was the Gramercy Park house and outside stood a policeman. The legend ran, "Guards protecting the Burketts from the maniac, Potter."

"I'll get in." Mr. Potter grinned confidently at them and went back down the circular staircase and let himself out of the church. He made a mental note to see that the kindly pastor was rewarded for the sanctuary he had unwittingly provided them.

Again he plunged into a crowded subway, got out at Fourteenth Street and walked up

239

Fourth Avenue. As he passed the delicatessen where he bought his beer, Phil, the proprietor, was standing in the doorway. In the past, when the house and the weight of the Burketts had become too much for him, Mr. Potter had escaped to the delicatessen where Phil had discussed the merits of the various Brandenberg concertos, Proust and impressionist paintings while he got out the beer. It had provided a pleasant and stimulating contrast to genealogy.

Phil caught sight of him, his eyes widened and he shook his head in warning. He turned to speak to the shopkeeper from next door. Behind his back his expressive hands signaled frantically.

Mr. Potter, whistling, "Who's afraid of the big bad wolf," went past, turned the corner, and walked toward the park. He crossed the street to the iron railing and started along the west side of the park, glancing casually toward his house. Standing very erect beside one of the big lamp posts that distinguished it from its neighbors, was a policeman, engaged in conversation with Tito, who had come up from the areaway.

Tito saw Mr. Potter, looked at him without any sign of recognition, and Mr. Potter went on around the park. By the time he reached the south gate, he settled down to wait as

240

patiently as possible. The area was almost deserted except for a bus that lumbered past and went down Irving Place. It was too early in the morning even for Adam Faber to be taking up his usual stand outside the Players.

Five minutes later, Tito, carrying a shopping basket, came up and slipped the key in the lock. He went in without a glance at Mr. Potter but he left the gate ajar. A moment later, Mr. Potter slipped in behind him. Tito was waiting in the shadow of Edwin Booth, where the policeman could not see him.

Quickly, Mr. Potter told Tito what he wanted. Tito set down the basket to give himself more scope and then flung out his arms.

"You're crazy to come here, Mr. Potter! You'll be arrested. There's a cop on duty, day and night. Anyhow, even if you come in the back way, you can't get upstairs. Mrs. Burkett is in the drawing room and Miss Burkett is shut up in the library talking to Mr. Fullmer. You'd never get down the hall past those two open doors without being caught."

"I've got to get in," Mr. Potter told him patiently, and Tito, with a look of tragic despair, capitulated. "Tell Antonia to be on the lookout for me and then you go around to Phil's and get enough food for three people for at least two meals."

Ten minutes later, Mr. Potter went through the alley. A workman, rolling ashcans out of the Fourth Avenue building, paid no attention to him as he slipped through the broken hedge into the garden. The house door was ajar and he went inside. The workman waited until the door had closed behind him and then darted into the building where he dialed a number and talked fast.

There was no one on the basement floor and Mr. Potter went up the uncarpeted steps as quietly as he could. The doors to the drawing room and library were open but so was the kitchen door. Antonia stood at the sink, watching him. She beckoned and he slipped into the kitchen, closing the door behind him. The swing door to the dining room was shut.

Antonia glanced at it. She was white with fear. She touched his arm as though to reassure herself that he was all right.

"Making a refugee of you in your own house," she whispered. "That's what they are doing. And ordering me around all the time as though I were dirt. And saying that as soon as the place is legally theirs, Tito and I have to go. We'd have cleared out already only we knew you'd come back and it would be better for you if you had some friends in the house."

"Friends," Mr. Potter said gravely. He patted

her shoulder. "How can I get upstairs?"

"You can't," she said promptly. "Mrs. Burkett is in the drawing room and Miss Burkett and Mr. Fullmer are talking in the library."

"Then," he told her, "you'll have to do it yourself. I need shaving things and clothes for myself and a friend of mine. He's a bit bigger than I am but they'll have to do. And clothes for a girl. You'll know what a girl would need. Can you get them from Miss Burkett's room?"

"The girl they had the pictures of in the paper?"

Mr. Potter nodded.

"Didn't look to me as if she wore 'em." Unexpectedly Antonia chuckled. "Do you good," she said. There was a step in the hall. "Mrs. Burkett! Coming to check up on the refrigerator. Afraid I'll waste her food. Get into the dining room but be careful they don't see you from the library."

Mr. Potter eased himself through the swinging door into the dining room. There was a closet for table linen and silver and he slipped inside, leaving the door ajar so that he could breathe.

He heard his Aunt Prudence's querulous voice saying, "How do you manage to spend all morning washing dishes?"

Antonia mumbled a reply and went out of

the kitchen, up the stairs to the second floor. Mr. Potter could hear her moving around in his room overhead and hoped Aunt Prudence would not go up to investigate. But she was busy in the kitchen, rummaging through the refrigerator, muttering to herself that she distinctly remembered there were three bananas, about scandalous waste and the general iniquity of Italians.

And from the library came Deborah's high, girlish voice. "...so I didn't know what to do. I realize that Hiram's out of his mind, but I thought you ought to be told, you ought to be warned."

"I am more than grateful," Fullmer said warmly, with that special gentleness he used for women. "Of course, as you say, it's insanity for Potter to try to claim that either Wagstaff or I is guilty of your brother's death and the killing of that poor girl. But a desperate man will grasp at a straw."

Deborah had begun to sob. "I couldn't bear it − to have any relative of mine do or say anything that might harm your career. I've been so − proud of you!"

"How very kind you are," Fullmer said again in that rich orator's voice that was always a bit too big for the occasion. "Sometimes I've felt−" there was a little pause − "you have so much understanding of what I am trying to accomplish. More understanding than — that means a lot to me. Encouragement and sympathy; a man needs them if he is to do his best."

"After all," Deborah said sweetly, "Pat means well, you know. We shouldn't condemn her. She can't help being superficial. But I'm afraid she won't enjoy being a politician's wife. She doesn't understand the obligations. She's not used to — being careful about what she does and says. She's not bad; she just doesn't think. It worries her father a lot; I remember how upset he was when she married that gangster."

"When she — *what!*" Fullmer said explosively.

"Oh," Deborah said with a little gasp, "I didn't mean — I supposed of course you knew. I never dreamed that Pat would get engaged to you without telling you she had been married before."

"Pat married?" Fullmer sounded bewildered. But Fullmer, like all good orators, was part actor. Mr. Potter wondered how much of his shock and surprise was genuine.

He found himself shaking with rage. For the first time in his life he longed to use violence against a woman.

"Bernard," she went on, sounding like an ingenue of the Mary Pickford vintage, "you mustn't mind too much. If you really love her,

245

she will be worth even giving up your career."

"Giving it up?" Fullmer was aghast.

"I know. I know what—" she faltered — "what love is. Though it is a tragedy because you could be so useful to your country, so important — there's no limit, really."

Fullmer was shaken. "Deborah, are you sure about Pat?"

"Why, of course!" From his vantage point Mr. Potter could see their figures distorted by the rounded front of the glass china closet. Deborah's hand was on Fullmer's arm, reaching for his coat lapel. "Since we've known about poor Hiram, that his mind has gone and the property will come to us, I've thought more than ever before about the responsibility of money. A girl like Pat might be tempted to use it selfishly—" she let the thought finish itself in Fullmer's mind.

"Deborah," Fullmer said again, a change in his voice.

"Oh, my poor Bernard!" She let her head droop against his shoulder, as though drawn by an irresistible magnet. His arm went around her. She raised her mouth. Fullmer bent over and kissed her.

"I'm sorry," he said. "I was carried away. I shouldn't have done that but you were so kind — so sweet — Deborah—"

"Oh, Bernard!" Deborah's arms linked around his neck, like a chain he'd never be able to break, Mr. Potter thought with a little glow of satisfaction. "Oh, Bernard!" She could not prevent the triumph from ringing in her voice.

Chapter 16

Opal emerged from the bathroom in the little apartment in the church tower and turned around slowly for inspection. It was not, Mr. Potter discovered with pleased surprise, Deborah's clothes that had been at fault. It was Deborah. In a knitted suit of pale lavendar Opal stopped the breath. She had restored her familiar make-up, increased the heavy scarlet line of her mouth, the mascara and blue tinge of her eyelids. The knitted suit clung tightly to her breasts and outlined the small rounded stomach.

"It's too tight," she said dubiously. "I guess Deborah didn't—"

"Deborah didn't," Mr. Potter agreed enthusiastically.

"Well, anyhow, it's just the sort of thing I need right now."

Something in her voice made Sam demand,

"What are you up to, sugar?"

For once the forthright Opal was evasive. "Oh, I've got a sort of idea I'd like to try out." She took a cigarette from Sam. Behind the grotesquely artificial make-up her eyes were steady and clear. "You two keep thinking it must be a man who killed Jennie and Thomas and Mrs. Newcomb. But I can't help believing this Deborah is in the business somewhere. When you come down to it, Bernard Fullmer is the ambitious one, the one with the most to lose if anything got out about him; he's the one who had an appointment the night Jennie was killed. And your cousin Deborah is in love with him and just as crooked as her brother, if you ask me, the way she's trying to get him."

She leaned forward so Sam could light her cigarette. "Look at it this way, Hiram. Your family is trying to throw the blame on you for all this killing, though anyone knowing you — well, that makes liars of them, doesn't it? After all, Sam didn't see anyone leave the house the night someone got in to Thomas's room. So that makes a thief of Deborah, doesn't it? And now, she is trying to get Fullmer, holding a gun to his head, but I'm blest if I know whether she is warning him that she knows he is guilty or whether she's holding out the Potter money as bait and trying to scare him off the Wagstaff

249

girl because of scandal. Anyhow—" She crushed out the cigarette into a heavy glass ashtray and slipped into Deborah's light camel's hair coat.

"Hey, where are you going?" Sam asked in alarm.

"I won't get into any trouble." Opal sounded confident. "This is something only a woman can do and I promise to be careful. I'll be back in a couple of hours at the latest." She waved her hand and closed the door behind her before the two young men could protest.

The settlement house was a neat brick building in the middle of the block, a much more modern, less haphazard affair than the one Opal had known as a child. Even the atmosphere had changed. There was no longer the stale air of charity to be breathed; this was a flourishing community house without stigma of any kind. From the big room at the back came the sound of a tinny piano as the settlement worker played a nursery tune vigorously and small children scampered to its rhythm.

On one side of the main room a dozen or more women of all ages were learning to knit. The older generation dressed and thought according to old-country tradition; the second generation had already begun to make that intangible transition from the old to the new, not only outwardly but inwardly.

At a desk near the door sat Patricia Wagstaff, wearing a severely simple black suit with a crisp white blouse, her tawny hair hatless. Opal slipped off the coat which concealed her magnificent figure and walked up to the desk.

"Miss Wagstaff?" she asked.

The two girls examined one another with a frank, mutual curiosity.

Pat smiled. "What can I do for you?"

Opal dropped her eyes. "I guess I need to talk to someone," she admitted shyly. "Another woman. Only there's no point in talking to those old dames," and she glanced with the arrogance of youth at a couple of social workers who were tottering along in their middle thirties. "I've got to talk to someone my own age, who can understand."

Pat was interested. "Are you in trouble?" she asked, lowering her voice discreetly.

"Well — not a baby, if that's what you are thinking. Only there's a man who promised to marry me and — you know how it is — you get kind of carried away. And now he says he won't." Opal looked up quickly, looked down again, but in that brief glance she had seen what she had fully expected to see, the fascination which the fallen woman has for the respectable one.

"I'm terribly sorry," Pat said in her warm

voice. She pulled up a chair, the solitaire diamond flashing with many-colored lights as she did so. "Do sit down. Though I'm afraid there's no way I can help you. But sometimes it helps just to talk it out, don't you think?"

Opal nodded vigorously.

"This man isn't married already, is he?"

"Oh, no, I'm sure of that." Opal twisted her hands. "I guess I was sort of crazy to come. Only I thought — maybe if you would talk to him — well, like you could make him see I'd be a good wife. It isn't as though — the way I look at it, these society dames aren't so smart. It doesn't take so much brains to figure out how to do things right. I could learn etiquette and all that. And I'd try hard."

"You mean that this man is in society?" Pat was surprised.

"Well—" Opal bit her knuckle, paused as though in an agony of indecision, took courage from Pat's friendly sympathy — "well, I figured as you know him, he might listen to you."

Pat was startled. The tawny eyes widened and narrowed. "I know him?"

"I saw your picture in the paper the other day. You were with him."

The color drained out of Pat's face. Even her lips were like chalk. "My picture — with him?" The words came on two breaths as though there were not enough air in her lungs to handle a whole phrase.

Again Opal looked up and down swiftly. "Mr. Hiram Potter," she said.

Pat expelled a long, shaky breath. When Opal risked another look she saw that the color had come back to the older girl's face and the sparkle to her eyes. She was struggling to maintain the proper gravity but her lips twitched treacherously.

She leaned over the desk, looking at Opal with new interest. "I think," she said, "you must be Opal Reed. I've seen your picture, too." This time the lips curved into a delighted smile. She glanced at her tiny jeweled wristwatch and got to her feet. "Time I was leaving. Why don't you come along with me, Miss Reed, so we can have a real heart-to-heart talk?"

"Thanks a lot. You are real kind," Opal said.

On the street Pat hailed a taxi and the two girls were silent until they reached the apartment building on East Seventy-second Street. Opal looked wide eyed at the uniformed doorman who leaped forward to open the door, and then swept grandly past him, surveying the lobby haughtily as though it were something that had been offered to her and that she had rejected. Again Pat found it difficult to control her mouth.

253

The Wagstaff apartment, which occupied an entire floor, the wide polished floor boards and oriental rugs, the somber paintings, the luxurious furnishings, stopped Opal cold. She lost her hauteur and followed timidly when Pat passed the maid who opened the door and tossed over her shoulder, "Serve tea in my sitting room, Kathy. Ah — skip the tea and have Brewster mix us a shaker of Bacardis, not sweet. He knows how I want them."

Pat's sitting room was small and compensated for the fact that it faced north by gold drapes at the window which gave an illusion of sunlight and a good deal of yellow in the upholstery. A fire crackled in a tiny white grate. Pat flung her coat carelessly across a chair and tossed Opal's on top of it. She bent over to lay another log on the fire, the blaze seeming to be reflected in her hair. Opal, perched on the edge of a yellow-and-white striped satin chair, watched the older girl, the girl Mr. Potter so obviously loved, and questioned for the first time whether he would altogether approve of what she was doing.

Pat settled herself in a deep chair, her long legs stretched out in front of her, reached for a cigarette and pushed the box across the table. "That silver bird thing is a lighter," she said companionably.

In a few moments the pretty maid came in with a tray containing a beaded cocktail shaker, two small glasses, a bowl of maraschino cherries and one of salted almonds. She set it on the table and went out.

Pat shook the shaker, listened for a faint hiss, and poured the cocktails. "Here's to landing your young man," she said. "And how long have you known Hiram Potter?"

"Not very long," Opal said. It was, she thought, sort of hard to grope your way when you were lying and the person you were talking to knew you were lying.

"I can't believe it of Hiram," Pat said, her lips sober, her eyes dancing. "Treating a girl like that! You never can tell, can you?"

"Look, Miss Wagstaff." Opal settled herself more firmly in her chair and met the other girl's eyes levelly. "I was lying about Hiram, of course. You know him well enough to know that's ridiculous. But I had to talk to you and I couldn't figure out any other way to do it. If I'd just started in with what I have to say you might not have listened. And you've simply got to listen."

"Of course," Pat admitted, "I knew it was nonsense about Hiram. But you've been tangled up in a ghastly mess and I'm terribly sorry. The police are looking for you. I guess you realize that."

"We realize that," Opal said grimly.

"Where on earth did you vanish to? Have you all been together, you and this friend of yours and Hiram?"

"Hiram hasn't killed anyone, Miss Wagstaff. He couldn't of. But his family is going to do everything they can to try and prove he did."

"Where is Hiram?"

"I'm − not just sure," Opal said. She put down her cocktail glass. She never drank much because a model can't afford to. In any case, she did not want to take a risk of having her tongue run away with her. "The reason I came to see you, Miss Wagstaff, is because we've simply got to find a way of stopping his family from acting like they are doing. It's his money they are after. To get it, they'd hurt anyone, Hiram − or you−"

"Me?" Pat looked at her blankly.

Opal hesitated and then plunged. "This morning Hiram went back to his house. We all had to have clothes. He got sort of cornered and he was hiding in a closet in the dining room−"

Pat's control slipped. She rocked back and forth, laughter gushing from her like water from a fountain. "Oh, no, I can't bear it! Hiram cornered and hiding in a closet in his own house!"

Opal waited until the laughter had trickled to a stop. Something in her very lack of response to Pat's mirth helped sober the other.

"That's how we know what the Burketts are up to," Opal said flatly. "Hiram heard his cousin Deborah talking to some fellow named Fullmer." She kept her eyes on the hands resting on her lap. "This woman wants the money so she can marry Fullmer. She made him think if Hiram was proved crazy she'd have the money and he could spend it the way he liked to help along his career. She said Hiram was trying to prove either him or your father killed Jennie."

"But that's a lie!" Pat flamed.

"Well," Opal said slowly, "I guess, at that, it has to be one of them. It was someone who met Jennie in the park and used the Potter key to get in. There's no one else."

"But it can't—"

"And Deborah," Opal swept on hastily, "is trying to break up your engagement to this man Fullmer. She told him you weren't fit to be his wife because you'd been married to a gangster, and I don't know what all. Hiram was fit to be tied because he couldn't stop her and — well, anyone would know what Hiram thinks of you. But this cousin of his just twisted the guy around her finger. They were in each other's arms and he said she was the one who understood him, and all about how much his career mattered—"

"I don't believe it!" The words sounded like a cry of pain. Pat got up from her chair, tall, lithe, graceful. Her hands clenched at her side. "I don't believe it! Not Bernard. He loves me. He would never listen to Deborah." She walked to the window and back to the fireplace.

"He listened all right," Opal said flatly. "That's why I came to see you. The Burketts want Hiram's money, and his cousin wants your fiancé, and they won't stop at much to get what they want. I thought maybe together we could figure out something. After all, you know the Deborah woman and I don't."

Pat rested her arms on the mantel and dropped her head on them. She sagged, her body losing its grace and lightness and aliveness, a heavy inert burden. Opal waited, too sensitive to break in on a grief that was like despair. Her father or the man she loved – whichever choice Patricia Wagstaff made, it would be heart-breaking. She would have to be so terribly sure.

At length Pat's arms dropped to her sides and she came back to her chair. Her body still sagged, her face had a curious laxness, her eyes were empty. She rang the bell. The pretty maid appeared, looking rather flushed and straightening her disordered hair.

"Kathy, is my father — oh, I see he's back." Pat's dry tone caused some confusion on the maid's part. "Will you ask him if he will please come in here? There's someone I want him to meet."

She did not speak to Opal or look at her. Her head rested against the back of her chair as though she were too tired to move. Wilbur Wagstaff came into the room, looked questioningly at his daughter, his face tightening in concern when he saw her expression. He turned to Opal and brightened. Opal, who had seen that look too often in the faces of out-of-town buyers, was wary.

"Miss Reed," Pat said in a colorless voice, "this is my father. Dad, this is Opal Reed, the model who was with Hiram when he was arrested at the Gink Club."

Wagstaff's soft hand held hers, pressed it, relinquished it regretfully. "Well, Miss Reed, this is a pleasant surprise."

"Not so pleasant," Pat said, still in that sick voice. She repeated, quickly and accurately, the conversation she had just had with Opal. "And so Bernard is turning to Deborah, because she is so understanding, because—"

"Don't be absurd!" Wagstaff said sharply, his eyes searching his daughter's face, looking for some clue there that he failed to find. "Fullmer isn't such a fool as to turn from a girl like you to Deborah."

"Opal thinks he already has, that Deborah has poisoned him against me—"

"I'll have a talk with Fullmer at once. After all, he can't afford—" Wagstaff stopped quickly, shot a covert look at Opal and turned back to his daughter whose unhappiness upset him so. He started toward the white telephone on her desk.

"Wait!" Pat's voice held him. "Dad, I don't think you quite understand. Hiram believes that either you or Bernard killed those people. Why is Bernard so — frightened?"

There was something in the atmosphere that Opal did not understand, an undercurrent of disaster. She got up. "I guess I'd better go. Thanks a lot for the cocktail and for listening to me."

Wagstaff slowly took his hand off the telephone. For a moment he stood deep in thought. "Where is Hiram, Miss Reed?" he asked.

"I don't know," she answered steadily. "He brought me some clothes and went away again."

"Call down for the car, Pat," Wagstaff said. "I'll drive Miss Reed home."

"Oh, no," she said hastily. She was desperately eager to get away from the man with the cushiony hands and the cold eyes. She wasn't exactly afraid. Why fool herself? She was afraid. "You are very kind but I'm not going home yet. I have some shopping to do."

"Where can I reach you?"

Opal pulled on the camel's hair coat, her fingers fumbling awkwardly with the buttons, and edged toward the door. "I can't tell you right now. We're − sort of − hiding out. But I'll call you tomorrow."

"Dad, I want to speak to you for a moment," Pat said. "Please excuse us, Miss Reed." She went out of the sitting room followed by Wagstaff. He turned for a final look at Opal, then he closed the door behind him and Opal heard a tiny click as the key turned in the lock.

She did not wait to try it, she ran through the small bathroom into the bedroom. There were three doors, one on the main corridor which she did not bother to touch; the second was a closet door on which she wasted seconds; the third opened on a small hallway. She went out, closed the door behind her, dived across the hallway into a large linen closet and pulled the door almost closed. Footsteps came rapidly down the hallway and a key turned in the bedroom door.

When the footsteps had died away she pushed the door of the linen closet open, inch by inch.

261

At one end of the hallway there was a room evidently used as a sewing room in which two maids were talking. She peered out. Only one of them was within her range of vision and her back was turned. On tiptoe Opal went down the hall toward the main corridor. At least, she thought stoutly, they can't lock me up if I am found here. I can scream, can't I?

The corridor, too, was deserted. From behind a half-closed door she heard Pat's low voice and saw Wagstaff's dark coat sleeve. The Wagstaffs were in consultation.

"Bernard," Pat was saying in a hushed voice. "Don't you see — it has to be Bernard."

Opal opened the front door as silently as possible and let herself out. She kept her finger on the bell until the elevator arrived. Only when the door had closed behind her did she let herself drop onto the upholstered seat that ran across the back of the elevator. In its mirrored walls she saw her frightened face.

Chapter 17

"Well," Opal said defensively, "I can't see why you take it like that."

"I suppose not." Mr. Potter's very repression helped to convince her that behind the control of the quiet, fair-haired man there lay the devil of a temper.

"What else could I do?" she protested. "Anyone can see this guy Fullmer is guilty. Your cousin Deborah knows it and she is trying to cover up for him, to throw the blame on you and get your money — and him, too. He has to go along with her; he doesn't dare do anything else. As for the Wagstaffs, personally I agree with Sam. I think old Wagstaff is deliberately throwing you to the wolves to protect Fullmer, just because his daughter wants him. Well, I thought it was time to show them where they stood, that's all."

"But why in hell," Sam exploded, "did they lock you up?"

"I guess they were knocked off their feet and wanted to figure out something before I could tell anyone else. Wagstaff was hell-bent on finding out where you were, Hiram, and, if I'd told him, he'd have had the police here in two minutes, family friend or no family friend."

"What I can't understand," Mr. Potter said bitterly, "is why you had to borrow something out of the confession magazines to tell Pat that you and I—"

Opal looked guilty. "Well, I couldn't just barge up to her and say, 'The man you want to marry is a murderer.' She'd have had me thrown out of there. So I had to think of something to — sort of hold her interest and ease into it. Anyhow," she added kindly, "she didn't believe me, if that is any comfort to you."

Apparently, it was of small comfort.

"I'll tell you this much, Hiram," Opal declared. "If you'd just let people see what you're like under the surface, you could get any girl interested. Any girl."

"And that," Sam told her, "will be about enough from you."

Again Opal gave him an eager, questioning look and, finding nothing but friendly amusement in his face, the light faded from her eyes.

"What I would like to know," Sam admitted, "is what has this guy Fullmer got that makes women go off the deep end about him?"

All three were deep in thought. Sam was the first to come to a decision. "One thing, we are sure the guy is our murderer and everyone is trying to cover for him. We've got to prove it before he gets us." He pulled out a crumpled cigarette package, prodded it in, twisted it up and looked around the room. Automatically, Mr. Potter reached in his own pockets. They were empty. He went over to the couch where his gray suit was lying, felt in his pockets, tossed cigarettes to Sam, and pulled out a small address book. He turned it over in surprise.

"Oh," he said, "that's Thomas's. I'd forgotten all about it. It was in his desk drawer with that money."

The other two looked up alertly and stood, one on either side of him, while he turned the pages.

"My, my," Opal exclaimed, as he scanned each name and looked at the comment under it, "what a man!"

"What a list!" Sam added. "How's about letting me copy some of those names?"

"Just try it," Opal warned him.

Under the F's there was a notation: B. F., an address on East Twenty-second Street and, under it, in parentheses, the words, "Jennie Newcomb." It was followed by a series of exclamation points, and a large underlined dollar mark.

"Jennie!" Mr. Potter said.

"We've got the bastard," Sam breathed fervently.

"Let's go," Opal said.

"We can't all go," Mr. Potter pointed out. "If one of us is arrested, someone has to be free."

After considerable argument it was decided that Mr. Potter and Opal would go to the Twenty-second Street address and Sam was to remain behind. If they had not returned within two hours he was to take action. Mr. Potter wrote down a list of lawyers from which the name of Wilbur Wagstaff was conspicuous by its absence, but he yielded only reluctantly to having Opal accompany him.

"I'll be the decoy," she insisted. "I'll keep Fullmer busy while you look for traces that Jennie worked there."

As tactfully as possible, Mr. Potter suggested that Opal was hardly the right kind of decoy to attract this particular duck. She was not offended. Instead, she looked over the clothes Antonia had stolen from Deborah and selected a dull-looking gray-linen dress with a severe white collar; a dress, Mr. Potter remembered, in which Deborah had contrived to look like a missionary after some years of wearing service. Opal disappeared into the bathroom and when she emerged the make-up was gone, her hair hung loosely around her face. Even this dress failed to extinguish her; it made her look like a demure schoolgirl and, because of its loose fit, the spectacular lines of her body were properly submerged.

"That ought to do it," she said in a tone of satisfaction, "though I must say he is the most virtuous murderer I ever heard of."

Sam checked his watch by Mr. Potter's and kissed Opal good-by. "Look out for the kid," he said. "I don't want her running into any more trouble. She's had enough because she knows me and knew Jennie through me." He groaned. "If she keeps on like this, I'll have to end by marrying her."

"You might as well get used to the idea," Opal told him. "That's exactly what I intend you to do, as soon as you settle down."

The address on Twenty-second Street was not far from Gramercy Park but it belonged to a different world, a noisy commercial street lined with warehouses and filled with trucks. Wedged between the larger buildings was a small brownstone with a worn stoop. In the lobby there were half a dozen cards: Finkelstein, Smith, Graham, Morella, Bayard, Hastings.

"Bayard," Mr. Potter said at once. "Though of all the insufferable — unless he has had his tongue in his cheek all the time."

He rang the bell marked Finkelstein, waited for a click, and when there was no response he tried Smith. After a moment the inner door clicked open and they went into a narrow hallway with linoleum on the floor, an uncarpeted stairway and an unshaded drop light. The apartments on this floor were occupied by Finkelstein and Graham. On the second floor, the cards read Morella and Hastings.

The back apartment on the third floor was marked Smith. As they reached the top a woman in an elaborate robe peered out. She did not see Opal, who was behind Mr. Potter.

"Busy now," she said in a low tone. "You'll have to come back later." She closed the door.

"Well, well," Opal whispered. "Nice company Bayard the Peerless keeps. And I have to doll up like the Salvation Army for him."

The front apartment bore the card Bayard. From inside came the sound of hasty movements, followed by a spate of hammering. Under cover of the sound Mr. Potter eased open the door. Bernard Fullmer, coat off, necktie loosene , sleeves rolled up, was hammering shut the top of a wooden crate.

The apartment consisted of two small rooms

which had been converted into offices, meagerly furnished with cheap desks, chairs and filing cabinets. The cabinets were open and papers were stacked on the desk. Fullmer was rapidly packing them.

Mr. Potter stepped into the room, Opal crowded in behind him and closed the door. Fullmer straightened up with a jerk. As he caught sight of Mr. Potter the color faded from his face and his hand tightened around the hammer. He poised lightly on his feet, ready to launch himself at the intruder, holding Mr. Potter's eyes with his own. Instead of hurling himself forward, however, he edged backward, his free hand groping for the telephone.

"Let the telephone alone, Fullmer," Mr. Potter warned him.

Opal stepped out from behind him, demure and childlike in the gray dress, her big eyes fixed on Fullmer's face. "So you are Bernard Fullmer," she said, her voice soft but filled with a kind of delighted surprise. "Now I can understand it."

Mr. Potter tilted his head a little on one side, a glint of humor in his eyes while he watched her. Fullmer was at a loss. Confronted by the girl's obvious admiration, his belligerent attitude was incongruous. He put down the hammer and reached for his coat, summoning up his most winning and sincere smile.

"What's all this about?" he asked. He turned from Opal to Mr. Potter, still wary but more perplexed than alarmed. "Look here, Potter, I suppose you know the police are looking for you. I don't like to be inhospitable or anything like that, but I'd appreciate it if you'd get out."

Mr. Potter smiled. "But where can I go?" he asked reasonably. "After all, I have no hide-away, no secret office—"

"There's no secret—" Fullmer began and stopped.

"No?"

Fullmer was annoyed by the quizzical arch of Mr. Potter's brows. "How on earth did you manage to run me down here?"

"I found the address in my cousin's address book."

Fullmer was embarrassed. "Deborah?"

"Thomas," Mr. Potter said coldly.

"Look here, Potter," Fullmer said with an attempt at sincerity that did not quite come off, "Deborah tells me you have some crazy—" he broke off as though the word were untactful — "some wild idea that I had a hand in her brother's death." He seemed to find Mr. Potter's steady gaze unnerving. "There's no truth in it, but I'm sure you know that. If your cousin had any knowledge of this place, he never even hinted it to me."

"What goes on here, anyhow?" Mr. Potter asked. As he moved forward, Fullmer moved back, watching helplessly while Mr. Potter took up stacks of pamphlets. "Campaign headquarters," he answered his own question. "But why keep it so — oh." He was looking down at handwriting he recognized. He had seen it for years on Wagstaff's monthly reports on the state of Potter's investments. He felt as though he had sustained a blow. "Oh, so Wagstaff is backing you *sub rosa*, is he?"

"I can explain it to you," Fullmer said eagerly, "but it would be difficult to explain it to the voting public. Mr. Wagstaff knows how Pat and I feel about each other. After all, I am — I was going to be his son-in-law and he wanted me to do well for her sake. Pat persuaded him to help me financially with the campaign. Naturally, he can't — he couldn't come out in the open because my campaign is based on cleaning up the gambling and racing rackets."

It occurred to Mr. Potter that Fullmer was having some difficulty with his tenses. The latter fixed limpid eyes on Mr. Potter's face. "And I mean that," he said in ringing platform tones. "But if people were to know where the money for my campaign comes from, they would question my sincerity."

271

"It looks to me," Mr. Potter said, "as though the office were breaking up. What's the big hurry?"

"What it amounts to is this." Fullmer settled himself on the edge of the cluttered desk, hands clasped around his knee, handsome face turning from Mr. Potter to Opal. "I don't want any more of Wagstaff's help. A man can pay too heavily for that sort of thing. This morning I saw your cousin Deborah and realized that Wagstaff — well, he seems to have a motive for killing Thomas and Jennie Newcomb. They knew something about Pat that he didn't want me to know. So—"

Seeing Mr. Potter's expression, Opal thrust herself in front of him and forestalled him by speaking quickly. "So you are the man Jennie thought was so wonderful!"

Fullmer smiled at her, turning on her the full battery of his charm. "Did she?"

"When did she come here to work?"

"A few weeks ago. Wagstaff brought her in. Treated her as though she were his own daughter. You know, when you establish informal friendly relations with your employees, they'll work their hearts out for you."

Again Opal forestalled Mr. Potter. She began to feel as though she were holding back an enraged dog and wondered how long she would be able to hang on to the leash. "But why," she asked breathlessly, "didn't you say anything when she was killed?"

"I didn't know who she was. I swear that by Almighty God. I hadn't the faintest suspicion; there wasn't any association between our office girl and the one who fell out of the office building that I knew of. But when Potter told us about talking to her in the park, told us her name, I was worried. Mighty worried. And yet, I had absolutely nothing to do with her death. I didn't see why I should be penalized, my career—"

"If I hear you use that word again," Mr. Potter said softly, "I'm going to push it down your throat."

Fullmer involuntarily took a step backward and wiped his head. "I know you don't like me but you can't ruin my—" he broke off hastily — "damage my whole life for something I don't know a thing about."

"You withheld vital evidence from the police. How do you think they'll like that? I suppose you realize the existence of this office will come out, the fact that Jennie worked here, the fact that your father-in-law elect backed you secretly while pretending to oppose you, just as you claimed to oppose everything he stood for while taking his money."

"Listen, Potter." Fullmer's face was deathly white and strained. "I've worked like a dog to get where I am, and I did it honestly. I never knew the girl outside this office. Why should I smash my whole life for her? Can't you give me a break on this?"

Mr. Potter made no comment but his expression of contempt made Fullmer wince.

Opal asked, "Did Jennie leave anything here?"

Fullmer answered almost eagerly, "Her desk is the little one in the other room." He watched while Opal went through the desk. In the bottom drawer there was a box of powder from the five and ten, a lipstick and a small broken comb. Nothing else.

"Be careful," Mr. Potter warned her as she reached for them. "Her fingerprints may be on them. Stay where you are, Fullmer! Hands off! I'm tired of being hounded. I'm going to get to the bottom of this ghastly thing. Three people have been killed and the thing has to stop."

Fullmer wiped his head and the palms of his hands. "I swear to God, Potter, the publicity—"

"Damn the publicity!"

"For God's sake, Potter," Fullmer said desperately. He clutched at the other man's arm. "You must realize I knew nothing about this. I'm not to blame if Wagstaff went haywire."

"Would you let your father-in-law go to the electric chair without a single gesture to help him?" Mr. Potter asked with detached curiosity.

"After Deborah's revelations," Fullmer said, "there is no further question of marriage with Pat. I checked up at the license bureau and found she really was married, though she never told me. I sent her a letter by messenger an hour ago."

Mr. Potter's unregenerate heart leaped at the thought of his beloved's heartbreak. At least, she would be free — free.

"Are you planning to marry Deborah?"

Fullmer hesitated.

Mr. Potter grinned at him with wicked mockery. "You'll have one hell of a time getting me committed as a mental incompetent," he said cheerfully. "Even with Wagstaff's help. And I doubt, under the circumstances, if you can count on any more help from him. So if it's the Potter money you're interested in, you had better try your luck elsewhere."

A scream from the outer office sent the two men bolting through the doorway. Opal stood beside the desk, her finger pointing at the telephone pad. "Hiram! Look! Look!"

He followed her pointing finger to the memorandum pad. The page was blank but someone had written so hard on the page that had been torn off that the impression had gone through. It was a Hackers Point telephone number, with the name Newcomb scrawled in Wilbur Wagstaff's handwriting.

Mr. Potter straightened up. He had come to the end of the road and found what he had feared to find.

"We'll leave the place as it is. Are you coming with us or will you wait for the police, Fullmer?" He lifted the telephone and called the police. "We had better move fast," he told Opal.

Fullmer went out ahead of him and Mr. Potter locked the door. He dropped the key into his coat pocket.

Chapter 18

A police radio car was threading its way among the trucks on Twenty-second Street by the time they reached Broadway. Mr. Potter checked himself as he was about to hail a taxi. The subway was safer.

"Coming with me?" he asked Fullmer.

"Where are you going?"

"To see Wagstaff."

Fullmer could not quite meet his eyes. "Under the circumstances—" he began.

Opal slipped her hand under his arm. "Mr. Fullmer and I will be waiting for you," she promised, and she led the unresisting man down Broadway. Mr. Potter wondered what Fullmer would think of the hide-out on the Bowery and then forgot him completely.

He emerged from the subway and walked west along Seventy-second Street. In Central Park the trees were still bare. For a moment a couple of horseback riders were silhouetted against them and then moved on. An attendant from one of the big apartment buildings went by, gaudy in gold braid and buttons, self-consciously walking a couple of dogs. They sky was a deep cloudless blue, offering a promise of spring that was not fulfilled by the chilling air.

At Madison Avenue, Mr. Potter hesitated. Even if the police were not watching the place, the doorman would have seen the newspaper stories. He knew Mr. Potter well by sight and he would not dare admit him.

In a Madison Avenue shop he bought a steamer basket of fruit. As he walked toward the apartment house his heart accelerated its beat. Across the street a taxicab was drawn up before the entrance to a building, the flag up, waiting for a passenger. In front of the building in which the Wagstaffs lived, a couple of tree surgeons were fastening ropes and tackle to an anaemic tree that was trying to survive a diet of exhaust fumes. The doorman was standing inside the entrance talking to a young man who faced the street but paid no attention to Mr. Potter. The latter ducked down the steps to the service entrance below the street level and rang the bell, keeping his back toward the main entrance.

"Wagstaff," he mumbled and went toward the serv-back hallway. The door was opened by the cook who glanced from the basket of fruit to Mr. Potter and beyond to the elevator man, a question in her eyes.

"I'll take it myself," Mr. Potter said and walked past her, through the kitchen and dining room and into the broad main corridor.

There were voices coming from Wagstaff's study. He went inside and set down the basket of fruit. Pat and her father broke off their conversation, staring at him, unbelievingly. Wagstaff was slow to react to the situation. He had become an old man, vague, fumbling, uncertain.

Pat raised her head and looked at Mr. Potter, as though he were a shadow moving through a dream. She opened her lips to speak, made a helpless gesture with her hands and turned to her father.

"Don't touch that telephone, Mr. Wagstaff!" As the pudgy hand drew back slowly, Mr. Potter warned him, "I won't go to the electric chair for you. I won't even raise a hand to help you. Not even for Pat's sake."

He sat down, a slim, elegant young man with unexpectedly alert eyes. "So far," he went on, watching the older man, "the game has been all in your own hands. But we've found the connection between you and poor Jennie Newcomb, we've visited the office from which you were financing Fullmer's campaign, and found not only evidence that Jennie worked there but of your telephone call to Mrs. Newcomb. You moved fast, didn't you? When the police began to investigate Jennie's death, you got her step-mother here to call them off by proving it was suicide. When I blocked that, you made use of the Burketts' desire for money to try to prove I was off my rocker; advising me to run for it rather than face a psychiatrist."

"Good God," Wagstaff said at last. "Hiram, what are you thinking? It's not you – it's Fullmer–"

Mr. Potter shook his head. "Fullmer won't go to the chair for you either. He'd sell you out in a minute to save his own skin, to protect his career–"

"Yes, he would," Pat said unexpectedly. She was dry eyed. She had no more tears to shed. "We know that now. I – got a letter from Bernard a few minutes ago. He doesn't want to marry me any more. He – Dad and I have been talking. I was wrong about him. I thought he was wonderful. And he's just a killer–"

"No, Pat," Mr. Potter said gently. "Fullmer isn't the killer."

Her hand clutched at his arm. "But it has to be Bernard, you see. It has to be. There wasn't anyone else to take the park key."

"There was someone else," he said steadily.

The snub-nosed revolver was in Wagstaff's hand. "Self-defense," he said. "I got a permit for this yesterday. Protection from a maniac. Self-defense, Hiram." He addressed the younger man but he seemed to be convincing himself. He lifted the weapon with quiet determination but his face was purple, his forehead beaded with drops of moisture. "Pat, go to your own room, my darling."

"No," she said in a queer voice.

"Go away," he implored her, with anguish in his tone. "I've got to kill him. There's no other way. Go to your room."

"No," Pat said again, still in that queer voice, "I want to stay. I want to see you do it."

Mr. Potter had not moved. He did not move now. Slowly the barrel of the gun lifted and he welcomed it. He wanted to be dead.

"All right, Mr. Potter," said a voice from the doorway. "He won't pull that trigger now. Not before a witness."

Mr. Potter raised his eyes from the barrel of the revolver and saw the familiar features of O'Toole, the radio car patrolman. The officer came into the room, holding a businesslike .45, and took the revolver from Wagstaff's unresisting hand. The lawyer leaned back in his chair like a spent runner, as though tired to the point of exhaustion and, embarrassingly, he began to cry.

O'Toole looked at him with a kind of pity. "I guess you did the best you could," he said, "only it wasn't good enough. Anyhow, leave her free and she'd probably try to kill again." He moved quickly and handcuffs clicked over Pat's slender wrist, fastening it to his own. And then the room was filled with men.

II

"You led me quite a chase," O'Toole said mildly. "But it has been interesting." Even out of uniform he was, in an indefinable way, a policeman. Perhaps it was the eyes that were tirelessly observant; perhaps it was the mouth that, for all its engaging smile, was firmly controlled; perhaps it was his posture, easily balanced, lightly poised, ready for disciplined action. He tasted the smooth, smoky scotch and nodded his approval.

A week had passed since the arrest of the Wagstaffs, a week spent by Mr. Potter in answering the questions of a tireless young assistant district attorney, in dodging reporters, in assisting his aunt to find an apartment and settling enough money on her for her support and Deborah's. She had gone without a word of protest, grateful that he did not refer to her attempt to prove him mentally incompetent, relieved to escape at last from his white face.

Even Deborah, realizing that Fullmer's interest in her had been as ephemeral as her chance of obtaining the Potter money, was quiet and subdued. Only when the last of her luggage was carried down the steps of the Gramercy Park house did she say, "You wouldn't believe me about Pat, Hiram, when I told you she was no good. But, remember, I told you so!"

The house was free of them now and Antonia sang at her work and tomorrow the painters would come to bring light and color and warmth to the bleak, gloomy rooms. Some day, Mr. Potter assumed, without really believing it, the place would be habitable; some day he would enjoy living here. Some day — when he no longer heard Pat's voice, high and thin, saying, "I want to see you do it."

For a week he had avoided both Sam and Opal. It had been bad enough, thrashing the matter over and over with the energetic young man from the district attorney's office. But at length he relented and let them come, accompanied, to his surprise, by O'Toole.

They sipped their drinks in a silence that

was broken at last by Sam who commented to O'Toole, "You are looking very pleased with yourself."

O'Toole grinned. "I got reason. I'm out of uniform. Detective. Though you led me right to it; all I had to do was pick up the clues you handed me."

"But I didn't know myself. I—" Mr. Potter stopped. If only Pat's voice would go away.

"You were headed the right way," O'Toole told him. "But you were so blinded by the girl you couldn't see what the facts meant. I'll bet your friends knew." He included Sam in this for the sake of politeness, but his eyes were pleasurably engaged with Opal.

She nodded. "I thought it might be the Wagstaff girl. Hiram didn't believe his cousin Deborah when she told him about that previous marriage but Sam and I looked it up at the license bureau. She'd married the Miller guy, all right. So I got wondering about her. She was infatuated with Fullmer who wouldn't dare marry anyone with a scandal about them because of his darling little career. So she was vulnerable for blackmail. And she had been spoiled all her life. She thought she had a right to anything she wanted."

Opal put down her glass and changed her position, providing another demonstration that she had all the qualities required in a model. "When I told her Fullmer was selling her out for Deborah I saw her face. She died. Right in front of me she died. It was like—" Opal groped for words — "like she knew her life was finished and she lived it all up in a hurry in a few seconds, growing old. Her body got heavy and sagging. She just — she turned into an old woman and she died."

Sam put his arm around her shoulders. "Getting fanciful, sugar."

"Maybe," she said, but she was not convinced. "She knew Fullmer could check on the marriage for himself; she knew it was over. So then she got to work on her father to victimize Fullmer. If she couldn't have him, no one could." Opal shivered. "I don't think," she said slowly, "I was ever so scared in all my life as I was then."

O'Toole shook his head at her. "You shouldn't have taken a chance like that." He finished his highball. "I can't help feeling sorry for Wagstaff. The girl is all he has and he's devoted to her. She has always been wild and headed for trouble because she's one of those people who never grow up, never accept the fact that they can't have anything they want. He's being careful about what he says, weighs every word, because he's a shrewd lawyer, and he's still trying to find a way out for her. But, when the evidence was shown him, he admitted that Pat had married a gangster without his knowledge or consent. He found out about it when your cousin Thomas Burkett," he glanced questioningly at Mr. Potter, "obligingly told him and threatened to pass the story on to a gossip columnist who paid him nice fees for little tidbits like that. Wagstaff paid up. Then he got the marriage annulled and began to keep a close watch on Patricia. He was worried about her.

"The trouble with the girl was that she was of age and he couldn't lock her up. Anyhow, he had his own private ways of amusing himself and they distracted his attention now and then. We got onto the next thing through that guy — what's his name — big man with the white hair who thinks he has to prop up the Players?"

"Adam Faber?" Mr. Potter said, beyond surprise.

"That's the one. He came forward with his testimony. He met the Wagstaff girl at a party at Morland's penthouse a year ago so he recognized her when she drove your sedan up to the house and he noticed the key was left in the lock. And we found a print or two of her fingers under the lid of the trunk. Only ones she missed."

Mr. Potter remembered the Wagstaffs and

Fullmer coming back down the steps as he had driven up in the yellow convertible. Adam Faber, attracted by the photographers, had drifted up and spoken to Pat. What had he said? Something about the fact that she'd probably be driving the yellow convertible soon.

O'Toole went on. "We got Morland on the phone in Paris. He remembered the party. Adam Faber was there and both the Wagstaffs and your cousin, Thomas Burkett. Morland said the Wagstaffs hadn't expected to meet each other there, definitely not a father and daughter kind of party. He didn't invite the girl. She came with a friend of his — quite a guy as I made out — and she was pretty well lit by the time her father arrived. Very embarrassing all around. The old man was upset and took her home. It was just a couple of days after that he withdrew twenty-five hundred dollars in cash from his checking account and gave it to Burkett."

O'Toole waited until Mr. Potter had refilled his glass. "Well, after the Morland party the Wagstaff girl seemed to calm down and the next thing she'd become engaged to that stuffed shirt, Fullmer. He stood for everything Wagstaff was against but the girl was crazy about him and her father thought maybe it would straighten her out to marry the guy.

"Fullmer has no money of his own so Wagstaff decided to back him. Because Fullmer was anti-gaming and Wagstaff has a lot of money in race tracks, he had to do it under cover. Anyhow, it wouldn't have looked well if people had thought Fullmer was profiting by a rich marriage. Wagstaff picked up the poor Newcomb kid because he didn't want to go on record by hiring someone through an agency. He used her for clerical work because she was trustworthy and wouldn't give them away."

"And she never would of," Opal wailed. "Pat didn't need to kill her. She never would of."

"I guess," O'Toole said, "Patricia Wagstaff wasn't the kind of girl who would understand loyalty. Anyhow, thanks to you and the address book you found, we know Thomas learned about that secret office. Probably he followed Wagstaff there. And we know Jennie worked there. Fingerprints all over the place. We've got the tie-in clearly enough.

"Burkett called the office and blackmailed Wagstaff. He wanted cash or he'd make public the fact that Wagstaff was backing Fullmer. Wagstaff was over a barrel. He had Burkett on his neck for life or Pat would lose Fullmer. So he said okay. And the poor Newcomb kid, working overtime, heard the whole thing. Wagstaff told Pat what they were up against and she said she'd talk to Jennie, appeal to her as woman to woman. She told Jennie her father would meet her in the park and give her a 'bonus.' She knew she could get in from your house and it would be dark. Then she told her father Jennie had promised not to say anything so all was well. He believed her.

"But after the funeral she told her father she was going with Fullmer, slipped into the park, took Jennie over to the office building for a quiet talk and—" his hands made a sudden brutal gesture that was unbearably graphic.

O'Toole drank his highball in long gulps. "Well, her body fell into the garden behind your house and your cousin recognized the girl and he knew what had happened. This time he didn't go to Wagstaff. He went straight to Pat. And the next morning she drew twenty-five hundred in cash from her bank, money which she tried to get back the night you found your cousin's body in the trunk of the car. That's when she returned the park key."

"But why," Mr. Potter spoke out of his bewilderment, "why did she ask me to take her out that night? She must have known I'd use the car."

O'Toole hesitated. At length he said cautiously, "Well, she is an odd sort of girl. Very odd. I think she wanted to − be there when you found it."

And again Pat said in an unrecognizable voice, "I want to see you do it."

O'Toole looked away from Mr. Potter's face and went on hastily. "You were shadowed after you left the police station and our men saw her come in through the garden. She didn't leave the house until daylight. Apparently she spent her time in that room for showing movies in the basement, looking for Thomas's negatives. He," O'Toole again looked uneasily at Mr. Potter, "he took pictures. Fortunately, she did not find them. They were in a file marked, 'World's Fair views'. That's what she was looking for up at your cottage in the country."

Opal took a professional interest. "What kind of pictures?"

O'Toole tried to find a delicate way of expressing it. "Not the kind people pose for – when they know they are doing it, that is. He had some of Pat –" he whistled.

"How deep was Wagstaff in all this?" Sam asked.

"He's not talking. I think, when Jennie died and he learned from Mr. Potter who she was, he blamed Thomas. He had believed Pat when she said Jennie would cooperate and he did not know that they had met in the park. But when Thomas himself was killed he knew the truth. From then on it must have been hell. He was frantic but he was hell-bent on saving his daughter if he could. That's why he suggested to Mrs. Burkett the possibility of Mr. Potter being mentally incompetent. We've got that from her. I guess she was kind of reluctant to talk to you about that. He was playing on her dislike for you and the fact that she wanted the money so bad. Then he told you to run for it—"

Mr. Potter shook his head. "I thought Wagstaff was covering for Fullmer on Pat's account, so my best chance was to stay free until I could figure the thing out for myself. Mrs. Newcomb must have known the truth and I intended to get it out of her, one way or another."

"That," O'Toole said, "is where you crossed wires. Wagstaff hoped to stop the investigation by making Jennie's death a suicide but you blocked his move and by that time he was committed to a woman who was as rapacious as your cousin Thomas had ever been. It's a damned good thing there was a tail on everyone. The Wagstaff girl was followed all the way to Hackers Point and back again."

"You know," Sam said thoughtfully, "I've been trying to figure out your part in this, O'Toole. As a radio car patrolman—"

O'Toole was embarrassed. "Well," he admitted reluctantly, "I had the wrong slant on

Mr. Potter. About every other day we'd get a call from this house: someone was loitering, someone had a radio too loud, someone was giving a party, the kids made too much noise in the park and there were some dirty little brats in there who had no right to be enjoying all that exclusiveness. And as he was the man of the family, I was doing a slow burn. I'd have given a week's pay just to see him trip up on something so I could haul him in."

He surveyed Mr. Potter cautiously but read nothing in his face but profound weariness.

"I had a long-overdue leave coming to me and I planned to take a trip to Atlantic City. I live at my sister's on Third Avenue and we were talking about the two deaths at your house when my oldest nephew piped up. He thought a lot of you. Seems you had been letting him and his friends into the park to play, giving them skates and stilts and I don't know what all. So I began to wonder. I'd heard Mrs. Burkett was saying you'd gone crazy. Maybe I wouldn't have gone ahead only I was sitting in my car trying to map things out when you let the kid in. Well," he added lamely, "I was on my own time anyhow, so I followed a hunch."

"You mean you followed us," Opal corrected.

"All the way," O'Toole agreed, smiling broadly. "And I hope you never come closer to drowning than you did that day you dripped water all over the library in Hackers Point. We were a regular parade: the Wagstaff girl in a Chevrolet she'd borrowed, then her escort, then you folks in the yellow convertible, and me bringing up the tail of the procession."

The pleasant face became grim. "That Hackers Point murder is the one she'll probably burn for. Her tail figured she was after the Newcomb woman. He lost her somewhere on the road and headed for the doughnut shop to cut her off. He was trying to get through the window when she let the old woman drop on the floor. Then you came along and caused a lot of trouble. I had a hell of a time persuading the Ohio police to let you get through after you took your friend right out of their hands. I wanted you free."

He looked at Opal and grinned. "I hope, by the way, you are free."

She looked in reproach at Sam who was beaming benevolently at them both. "Yes, damnit," she snapped.

Mr. Potter ignored this interchange. "What will become of the Wagstaffs?"

"That's up to the D.A.'s office and a jury. You never can tell about a jury. Not many women go to the chair. She might get a break as criminally insane and then recover later on.

Her father's as smart as they come and he'll use every trick of the law to help her. He's an accessory after the fact, of course, but he's also a father protecting an only child; half the jury would do it themselves. Seem to think they are justified in keeping the little killers in circulation.

"Not that it matters much to his daughter. She just doesn't care. She answered a lot of incriminating questions before her father was on hand to stop her. But she'll plead not guilty, of course."

"I kind of like to think," Opal said, "that Fullmer will lose the election when it comes out that Wagstaff was financing his campaign."

"Damned if he isn't a fighter," O'Toole said. "He's doing his best to turn it into an asset. She did all that killing for him and he's doing all he can to send her to the chair. He made clear to reporters today that he regards the whole situation with horror. He believes she should suffer the full penalty of the law. His attitude does more to underline her motive in killing to prevent him knowing about that previous marriage than any other evidence that could be brought against her."

"Some day when you and other minions of the law aren't looking," Sam said, "I'm going to have the fun of pushing his face in."

O'Toole grinned. "I won't see a thing."

Mr. Potter spoke suddenly. "Pat won't see me. I've tried twice."

"I told you," Opal said with unexpected gentleness, "most of Pat died when she knew she'd lost Fullmer. The dead don't care any more." She leaned forward, her hand on his. "But you're alive, Hiram. And you've got a lot ahead."

"What?" he asked bitterly.

Opal drew him to the window. "All that," she said.

He looked out at the park, at the windows across the way that were turning red with the sunset, trees showing their first tender buds. There was a muted restless sound of traffic. Outside the house life went on. Inside there was musty close air and the presence of ghosts. Mr. Potter flung the window open and let in the spring.

THORNDIKE PRESS HOPES you
have enjoyed this Large Print
book. All our Large Print titles
are designed for the easiest
reading, and all our books are
made to last. Other Thorndike
Press Large Print books are
available at your library,
through selected bookstores, or
directly from the publisher. For
more information about our
current and upcoming Large
Print titles, please send your
name and address to:

THORNDIKE PRESS
ONE MILE ROAD
P.O. Box 157
THORNDIKE, MAINE 04986

There is no obligation, of course.